VOLUNTEER GAP

C. David Gelly

This is a work of fiction. The characters, incidents, and dialogue have been created from the author's imagination and are not to be interpreted as real. Names, characters, places, and incidents are either the products of the author's imagination or are used fictitiously, and any resemblance to actual persons—living or dead—business establishments, corporations, events, or locales is entirely coincidental.

ISBN: 1542631440
ISBN 13: 9781542631440
Library of Congress Control Number: 2017900952
CreateSpace Independent Publishing Platform
North Charleston, South Carolina

Lulu…the journey continues…

If you don’t terrify people a little bit... then what’s the point?

Acknowledgments

To all of you who have read and enjoyed *Fancy Gap* and *Orchard Gap*, my thanks for your support and encouragement! *Volunteer Gap* is the third novel in the series. The fourth installment will be totally dependent on *you.* If you enjoy my work, please tell all your friends and family. Post a great review on Amazon, and post shout-outs about this novel on Facebook, Instagram, Twitter, Pinterest, and so forth. I truly depend on you to spread the good news, and if you don't, this could very well be the end of the series! Keep the faith as you journey to *Volunteer Gap*...and back!

Author's Note

Our country is torn by the forces of change—both good and evil. In many facets of our lives, from terrorism to police killings to politics, the fabric of our well-being is challenged daily. Yet, as we have in the past, we will come together as one to navigate these dangerous times.

In *Volunteer Gap*, the forces of good and evil collide. The power struggles of competing drug lords who control the drug trade in the mountains of Southwest Virginia affect the lives of innocent bystanders from all walks of life. While this is a work of fiction, it reminds us of the challenges we face as a free society.

My thanks go to the wonderful Mennonite families who live in Southwest Virginia, as well as those in the Blue Creek community in Belize. You are all truly amazing people!

—CDG

CHAPTER 1

The late summer drought had been no friend to Southwest Virginia. The endless days had crops roasting in temperatures consistently over ninety degrees, and air conditioners strained to take the edge off the raging inferno. There was no immediate hope for any cool air to swoop in from Canada.

Hope Showalter wiped the sweat from her brow as she closed the door behind her. She fumbled with her keys before she found the one that would lock the front door to the restaurant on Court Street in downtown Hillsville. The rest of the Mennonite women who worked with her had already gone home for the day, and she was the last to leave—as usual.

She exhaled as she thought of the many meals that had been cooked and served that day. While most days were busy, the steady stream of customers coming into the restaurant was as many as she had ever seen. Most came in to beat the midday heat. That thought soon passed as she weaved through the streets of Hillsville. She was on the way to her new home in Volunteer Gap.

The fourteen or so miles seemed longer than usual because the air conditioner in her ancient Ford van sputtered, sending only tepid air out of the vents while the fan blew on high. She soon reached over, cranked all the windows down, and felt some relief.

She took in the sheer beauty of the landscape along the Blue Ridge Parkway and thought of how blessed she was to live in such a beautiful place.

Hope was anxious to get home. Her daughter, Hannah, was staying with a neighbor because she had been sick that morning when Hope had left for work. Hope thanked her lucky stars that her neighbor Louise Bennett was retired, very fond of Hannah, and always willing to look after her.

Her ancient Ford van strained as she drove up the driveway to the A-frame she called home. Little clouds of blue smoke came out of the rusty exhaust pipe as the engine coughed to a stop. Hope sat for a minute before she looked toward her neighbor's house, and she saw Hannah running toward the van with a smile on her face.

"Well, looks as if someone is feeling better," she said, and Hannah jumped into her arms.

Hannah was a newly minted nine-year-old, and she was recovering from the loss of her father. Peter Showalter had died some twelve months earlier; an aggressive, indomitable form of brain cancer had overcome his strong Mennonite will and the treatments the doctors had thrown at it.

Hope had sold their small farm some six months after his passing because the memories there were too much for Hannah to endure. The Mennonite community had been supportive throughout the ordeal, and many suggested she should stay closer to their church and school in Hillsville.

In the end, Hope decided to move to the small community in Volunteer Gap, where she found the lovely little A-frame, which was just the right size for two people. While it was a little farther out of Hillsville and away from the restaurant she managed, she loved the neighbors and the beautiful rolling hills of the countryside.

"She has been delightful to be with today!" Mrs. Bennett yelled across the grass while standing in her doorway.

Hope waved as she replied. "My young child seems to have made a remarkable recovery today, if I do say so! Thanks again, Louise, for helping. You are a blessing!"

Louise Bennett waved and smiled as she went back into her house. Hope handed her house key to Hannah. "Now, go unlock the front door while I gather my things from the van."

Hannah took the key and skipped all the way to the front door.

Hope turned and gathered her shoulder bag from the passenger seat. She looked over the driver's seat and stared at the bench seat in the back. She soon realized the cashbox—which contained all the cash and checks from the restaurant—was not in its usual place. Within a moment, she was on her knees and looking to see if the box had fallen to the floorboard.

Her mind raced in reverse to all the usual steps she took to close the restaurant. She immediately knew that, in her fatigue, she had forgotten the cashbox in her small office at the restaurant. Her instincts told her Hannah was near.

"Why are you on your knees, Mother?" she asked with a quizzical look on her young face.

"Child, your mother made many mistakes today. Most were small and overlooked. But what I'm looking for, my dearest child, is the money box from the Pantry."

"Oh, Mother, you must be really tired. You never forget the money box," Hannah said, and she put her finger to her lips and smiled.

As Hope stood, she looked at Hannah. "I hope Mrs. Bennett fed you well 'cause we need to go back to the Pantry for that box."

Hope did not smile as she climbed back into the driver's seat and snapped the seat belt closed. Although more than two years had passed since local druggies had broken into the restaurant, she knew the cashbox should never be left at the Pantry.

She lost some of her angst when she looked at Hannah, who had strapped herself into the passenger seat and rolled her window down.

"Ready to roll, my favorite copilot?" Hope asked.

Hannah gave her the thumbs-up sign and smiled *from cheek to cheek.*

CHAPTER 2

The seventeen-year cycle for the cicadas had ended. The hot and humid evening sky was serenaded as the cicadas suddenly found their voices. Felix “the Duke” Estrada didn’t hear a single one as he shut the door to his Ford F-150 pickup truck. He was parked in an alley near Carroll Street and Pine Street. Rogelio Medina, simply known as “Roger,” watched from the passenger seat.

Estrada slowly walked by the telephone poles on Court Street and threw a pair of red Chuck Taylor All Stars up and over the low-hanging telephone wires. He watched as the laces caught the wires, dangled, and swung back and forth in the slight breeze.

Medina watched and gave him the thumbs-up. Four other eyes watched from another truck hidden in the alley. Tony Esquivel and Luis Solis rechecked their weapons but paid close attention to the long knives and butcher knife on the seat between them. Esquivel checked his watch and knew the expected prey was due in about fifteen minutes.

Estrada had arranged to meet with Bobby Joe Turner and Donnie “Honest” Akers, who were the leaders of local drug peddlers in Carroll County, Virginia. They controlled the market along the North Carolina border in Carroll County and Grayson County and beyond.

Joaquín Guzmán Loera, or "El Chapo," backed Estrada's organization. El Chapo understood that Carroll County worked well as the distribution point for a wide assortment of narcotics that flowed freely from there to larger metropolitan areas to the south, such as Winston-Salem in North Carolina and Roanoke in Virginia, as well as other large cities in both states.

The recent uptick in Latino activity did not sit well with the resident dealers, who were quickly losing market share. For six months, Turner and Akers had directed hits on several Latino players. After the killings, the locals lost many dealers in their distribution channels because the Latinos had gone seeking deadly revenge.

Local law enforcement simply lacked the resources to effectively deal with the sheer numbers of foot soldiers both sides had dedicated to that war. The US Drug Enforcement Agency, as well as the FBI, underestimated what was happening in Carroll County.

Leroy Jefferson, the newly elected sheriff of Carroll County, had his hands full keeping the peace because he was the first African American to be elected sheriff in all of Southwest Virginia, and some were not pleased.

None of that mattered to Estrada now. His only concern was to kill Turner and Akers. Doing so would wipe out any effective leadership the locals had. Estrada had drawn them to this meeting to discuss a cease-fire because too many were being killed on both sides. Turner and Akers both had taken the bait and were expected to show up. *If only they knew.*

* * *

Hope drove slowly down Court Street. Hannah peered up into the sky and saw the red sneakers dangling from the telephone wires. She had never seen anything like that before. She turned to point them out to her mother as Hope parked in front of the Pantry. In the approaching sunset, all of Hillsville's sidewalks were quickly rolling up.

In reality, Hope would have been as curious as her child if she had seen the sneakers. In her Mennonite world, she was far removed from the harsh realities of the drug epidemic in the area. She would not have recognized that the sneakers drifting back and forth in the evening breeze was a signal of an impending drug encounter.

Hannah followed her mother into the restaurant. Although the day was getting dark, Hope didn't turn on the lights. She saw the message light blinking on the restaurant's phone. She resisted the urge not to listen—but not for long. As soon as she picked up the phone, Hannah went to the back of the restaurant. She stopped near the back door since she thought she had heard voices in the back alley.

Outside, Estrada and Medina approached Turner and Akers, who had parked in the alley. After some moments of small talk, Turner and Akers relaxed. They believed the other two were alone. They never saw Esquivel and Solis spring from their hiding places.

They also didn't see little Hannah Showalter, who had stepped onto the back porch to see who was talking in the alley. By now, Hope had gathered the money box, and she saw Hannah on the porch. She was moving silently toward her daughter when she saw the men in the alley.

As she reached Hannah, Esquivel and Solis stabbed Turner and Akers; within moments, both men were lying motionless on the street. Estrada took the butcher knife from Solis and, with two quick swipes, cut off both their heads.

Hope was terrified, and she tried to cover her daughter's eyes. She wanted to back away from the porch and go into the restaurant, but fear kept her frozen in place. She prayed they wouldn't be seen. Her prayer was short lived. Hannah spun and hugged her, but the movement caught Estrada's eye. He turned and saw Hope and Hannah standing on the porch. It took him a moment to digest what he was seeing. Hope spun Hannah around and thrust her back into the restaurant. Inside, she fumbled to lock the door behind her.

Estrada and Solis quickly moved toward the door but could not open it. They started through the alley, heading toward the front of the restaurant. They stopped in their tracks when they saw a sheriff's patrol car come up Court Street. They stood still before quickly retreating toward their truck.

After the patrol car passed, Estrada and Medina's truck sped off in a different direction. Medina drove, and Estrada looked straight ahead. Medina said, "Duke, do you know who those *gabo* women were?"

He wiped the blood from his hands before he replied. "They are the religious people who run the Pantry. The tall woman had the little white cap on her head."

Medina looked straight as he drove. "What do we do about that, Duke? After all, they saw us."

Estrada slowly looked at Medina. "We find them, *my brother, and we kill them.*"

CHAPTER 3

He sat under the large oak on the grass by the solitary white cross marking a distant burial plot in Felts Memorial Cemetery in Galax. He had been there for hours in deep meditation, as was his way. Sweat dripped from his chin, and a large beetle clung to his T-shirt. Without opening his eyes, he reached around with his right hand and pinched the bug between his fingers.

Within a moment, he opened his mouth and placed the dead bug on his tongue. He closed his mouth and slowly rolled the bug in his gushing saliva. With one quick gulp, he swallowed, and then he licked beads of sweat from his lips.

His new Apple watch chimed a few notes from his favorite Bavarian chant. He knew it was time to leave. As he stood and stretched, he looked at the image that appeared on his watch. A video began but lasted only a few seconds. A voice said, "Now that I am gone, you must avenge my death. Deliver justice to those who took me." His face twisted in a wicked grimace as he looked at the grave and wiped away his tears.

His Harley started with a turn of the key, and he started off through the narrow cemetery paths. Within ten minutes, he was in the alley behind the building he owned in downtown

Galax. The garage door opened when he approached. He parked next to his truck in the garage.

He climbed the back stairs to the spacious top floor, which overlooked Main Street. Before entering, he pulled his iPhone from his pocket and opened the Nest app. He quickly disarmed the ten Nest cameras he used to protect his space when he was away or sleeping.

Once inside, he stripped off his sweat-drenched T-shirt and jeans as he walked into the bathroom. He stood in front of the full-length mirror and admired all his nakedness. Exercise and precise eating habits had maintained the trim and tone physique he demanded of himself.

Once in the shower, the warm and soapy water helped him relax; he felt the day's stress flow out of his body and into the drain below his feet. He felt his power swell as he stroked his lather-filled hands back and forth. His moment of release came quickly. After he toweled off, he slipped into his white terry-cloth robe and sat at his massive desk.

Three oversize computer monitors fired up and came to life after he offered the necessary verbal commands while his right thumb was in the fingerprint scanner. His evening's work as an independent app developer for Google was about to begin. He was heralded in the small cadre of premier software developers; he was considered one of the best in the business. His time at Harvard and MIT had served him well.

The tech world knew Alphonse Pickering was the best of the best. Yet no one really knew him at all. Al Pickering developed remotely, and he completely masked his precise location. Some suggested he lived in Palo Alto, California, while others swore he had an office in the Research Triangle Park in Raleigh, North Carolina. And that was exactly what he wanted them to think.

Many corporations and national and international government agencies had spent millions of dollars and hours upon hours trying to undo his masterful hacking jobs. Companies and individuals paid him millions to wreak havoc on their competitors, but his clients didn't have a clue who he really was.

The chances of anyone tracing him to the tiny downtown area of Galax, Virginia, were slim to none. He knew many had tried, but no one could cut through the labyrinth of defenses and identities he had set up to protect his home base and, ultimately, his true identity. Even the Russians had tried and failed.

He was an only child, and his parents had given him up for adoption. His adoptive parents abused him to the point that he ran away and joined the army when he was old enough. He served in the US Army Special Forces. That was where he met US Army Chaplain Reginald Santa-Cruz.

The good chaplain provided the emotional support and encouragement Pickering needed when he left the army and went to college on the GI Bill. He stayed in close contact with Chaplain Santa-Cruz, or Father Tony as he was affectionately known. Pickering legally changed his name to Tommie Cruz, but no one knew that.

Father Tony was the reason he had moved to Southwest Virginia. He was the father Tommie had never had. Tommie was ever so happy to provide his friend all the IT technical support he needed for all his parish activities—as well as those activities only known to a few.

Some twenty-four months had passed since Father Tony had abducted two children from the old hotel at Fancy Gap. It had been in the legendary fog that caused a massive pileup on I-77 at the Fancy Gap exit. He had helped Father Tony develop his untraceable Internet postings. Ultimately, Father Tony had been killed while trying to escape. Tommie would never forgive Quinn McSpain and Louisa Hawke for killing his father.

Those two helped the local sheriff and the Virginia State Police with the investigation. They tracked Father Tony down in a deadly pursuit. Father Tony had shot Louisa Hawke, but she survived. Tommie knew she wouldn't be so lucky when she was in his sights.

It took time for Tommie to understand that his father wasn't perfect. Father Tony's peculiarities with younger children were offensive to some, but Tommie believed Father Tony had never intended to hurt anyone.

Tommie stood and moved to the other side of his apartment. He said "open," and the door in front of him slowly opened. Dim, recessed lights came on as he entered. He sat in a chair in the center of the room and stared at hundreds of pictures carefully pasted to the walls.

Small racks of spotlights highlighted many pictures of a large man with a smiling face. Pickering smiled as he thought of the many moments he had shared with Father Tony. His blood pressure began to soar when he looked at the pictures of the man and woman responsible for his father's ultimate demise.

He also looked at a small bottle filled with a clear, faintly white liquid. It sat on the very middle of the shelf. The contents lay placidly in the bottom of the bottle, and the stillness seemingly reflected the many years the bottle had gone untouched.

He rose from his chair and moved closer to the wall. Anger welled in his mouth as he placed his right palm over the man's picture and his left over the woman's. The anger broke from his mouth in a seething flood. "Quinn McSpain, the time nears when you and your bitch, Louisa Hawke, *will be mine*!"

CHAPTER 4

Quinn McSpain pulled his Dodge Ram into the crowded parking lot at the deli in Fancy Gap. He checked his watch and saw the lunch hour was almost over. He looked around the lot, but Louisa Hawke's Volvo was not there. She had gone to Winston-Salem in the morning to get her hair done and to do some shopping at the Hanes Mall.

He was tired from the bike ride they had taken that morning on the Blue Ridge Parkway. They had left the house just before dawn and headed out toward Fancy Gap and the Blue Ridge Music Center. He loved that ride because the hills always challenged them.

However, he soon discovered Louisa was feeling frisky that morning and kept picking up the pace, especially on the uphill parts. He paid her back when his weight worked well with gravity—that is, when he tore down the steep hills.

He sat in his truck for a bit and thought of his new life with Louisa Hawke and all they had experienced together. He shivered when he relived the moment she received a gunshot wound inflicted by a madman who had been preying on two young children in Fancy Gap. He also shuddered to remember the deranged young biotech scientist whose altered GMO corn seed had killed so many.

Until she retired, Louisa had headed the FBI's Criminal Investigative Division, and he had enjoyed a storied career as one of the top corporate security operatives in the world. Quinn smiled as he tried to recall the most recent promise they had made to each other: never get drawn into an investigation that would threaten their tranquil lifestyle.

Quinn slid out of the truck seat and walked into the deli. A smile was on his face. He waved to Sharon, the manager, who smiled as he sat at a table in the back of the deli. He enjoyed visiting with Sharon whenever he visited the deli. He checked his iPhone and sent a text to Louisa, letting her know he was there.

He felt a presence close to his table, and he looked up and smiled as Sharon smiled at him.

"Well, handsome, this is a rare day. You're flying solo, and I can have you all to myself. Did you kick that gorgeous redhead to the curb?" she asked with a coy smile on her face.

"Now, girl, you know I just couldn't do that, suga'! But if I ever did, I sure 'nuff would be a courtin' the prettiest woman in all of Southwest Virginia, I declare!"

She blushed and said, "Now, Quinn McSpain, you have the next thirty minutes to stop all this! You are making a poor little country girl get all excited!"

Quinn couldn't contain himself, and he doubled up in laughter. Sharon took a napkin from the dispenser and wiped tears from her eyes. The older couple at the next table stopped eating and looked at them both.

As soon as they contained themselves, the front door of the deli swung open, and none other than Libby Thomas strutted in. Sharon and Quinn both looked to the front door as she entered. Sharon's jaw clinched. "Well, lookee here," she said. "The most famous woman in all of Southwest Virginia graces us with her presence."

A year had passed since Libby Thomas had become the most famous horse owner in the world. Many in the close-knit club of thoroughbred horse owners considered Libby a savvy woman—one who never let money stand in the way of what she wanted to own.

She had spent millions on horses that always seemed to be stacked with potential but ended up being short on wins. However, that all changed when her prized filly, Belle o' Fire, became the first filly to contend for the Triple Crown. After winning the Kentucky Derby and the Preakness, her filly came eye to eye with immortality, in Libby's quest to win the third leg of the Triple Crown at the Belmont Stakes in New York.

Libby stopped at the counter and looked around the deli. Her gaze stopped when she saw Quinn sitting at his table. As soon as she placed her order, she turned and walked to his table. She grimaced at Sharon and said, "You can leave now. I want Quinn all to myself."

Sharon didn't budge.

"Well," continued Libby, "this must be my lucky day! Quinn McSpain sitting all by his lonesome. So, tell me, did you finally tell your Louisa to take a hike?"

Quinn squirmed in his seat. "Why, Libby Thomas, it's been a while. I hope you are well."

Sharon, who harbored no loss of love for Libby, piped in and said, "Now, Libby, I just can't recall if I offered my condolences. I'm so sorry your little pony missed out on that Triple Crown thing." She then walked away with a smile on her face.

Libby turned beet red and seethed. She sat next to Quinn. "To hell with that bitch and all those motherfuckers who were ecstatic Belle o' Fire was fucked over at the finish by that bastard who bumped her at the wire! God, I still have nightmares about that race!"

Quinn was silent for a moment. "Listen, Libby, your horse did better than any filly in history. She was within a whisker of winning it all. I thought she had won it all. You have nothing to be ashamed of."

She shook her head. "That shitty moment will live with me to my grave. I was within a moment of being heralded as the smartest woman in the world of horses. In that second, though, I became only a rich bitch who almost had it all. And you know what, McSpain? I don't cotton to being second in anything!

"My life flashed in front of me in that second. Hey, I know I'm not the nicest human being on earth, but I just didn't deserve what was dished up to me on that day. No, sirree! It all slipped away in that solitary stinkin' moment! It was all a piece of shit!"

The two women at the table next to them stood in disgust and left.

Quinn sat still and didn't say a word for the longest time. "Listen, Libby, I can just imagine the pain you are still feeling. All your life was wrapped up in Belle o' Fire and her quest for the Triple Crown. But listen. You have a pretty good life. There isn't much you don't already have. If anything catches your fancy, you can buy it."

Libby wiped away a few tears that had started to flow down her cheeks. "That's bullshit, McSpain, and you know it. People hate me for my money and power. They smile as if they adore me, but in reality, they stab me in the back whenever they can. Most of these idiots don't know how much good I do for Carroll County! And you know what? They couldn't care less! Hell, some folks hate me more than they hate Donald Trump!"

Libby reached over and gave Quinn's hands a good squeeze and smiled when he smiled. Neither Quinn nor Libby saw Louisa walk in. Sharon smiled as she watched Louisa walk toward them quietly. Louisa stood in silence as Libby wiped away more tears.

Quinn was the first to see Louisa. He quickly slipped his hands from Libby's. Libby stopped crying, looked up, and found Louisa staring at her. After a long moment of uneasy silence, Libby let out a mighty laugh. "Well, I'll be dipped in shit! Isn't this just perfect? The FBI lady catches her boyfriend holding another woman's hands. Simply divine!"

Louisa kept her mouth closed and bit her tongue for a moment. Quinn rolled his eyes. He didn't know what to expect.

Louisa said, "Libby, I do hope you have gotten over the disappointment you have been living through. Well, you might not believe this, but Quinn and I felt your pain when Belle o' Fire didn't win it all. But look at the bright side: she did win the Derby and the Preakness."

Libby held up her hand. "Stop that bullshit, Louisa! You don't have a clue as to the living hell I deal with each day. My nightmare doesn't go away. I see each second of that last race in my dreams. And the ending hasn't changed a bit. Belle o' Fire will never win that miserable race. It just isn't fair!"

More tears streamed down her cheeks. Quinn and Louisa watched her in silence. Libby suddenly stood and gave them both an icy stare. "Sit down, Louisa, and don't worry about your man. He was really trying to feel bad for me. You two really do deserve each other. Now, get out of my way," she said, seething, and she brushed Louisa aside.

Louisa and Quinn, as well as the customers in the deli, watched her leave and slam the door. Everyone waited for a metaphorical pin drop for the longest moment, and then Sharon quipped, "Don't let the door hit you in the ass, darlin'! Dang! I hate it that she forgot *her lunch*!"

CHAPTER 5

Leroy Jefferson sat in his favorite rocking chair. He was on the front porch of his farm. This was his favorite part of the day—when day edged into night. He smiled as he put his book down and looked at Laneisha in the porch hammock. She was sound asleep.

While he took it all in, he knew everything could change in a moment. He loved his farm and the hours of enjoyment he gained from working the land. However, his day job as sheriff of Carroll County was overwhelming at times.

Sheriff Frank Pierce had retired, and the race to replace him had taken on a life of its own. Leroy was still mentally recovering from the election campaign, which he had suffered through many months before.

He had been pleased with his role as a captain at the sheriff's department of Carroll County. The compensation was good and was certainly supplemented by the revenue Laneisha earned. She was, after all, the most trusted tax consultant in Carroll County. The revenue and agricultural tax considerations from his farm also contributed.

The county's leaders had been split on whom they preferred to be the new sheriff. Leroy knew who could look beyond the fact he was African American. The smart ones backed him because they knew he was capable and trustworthy and honest to a fault. Sheriff Pierce had promised his support, as did many other county government officials.

The elected political leaders understood and learned from what had happened in Ferguson, Missouri. They understood the benefits of having a qualified and smart sheriff, and his being black was a huge plus for Carroll County.

But not all shared that view. The very thought of having a black sheriff irked a good many people who held the view that only a white man should be sheriff. They convinced Bobby Longo, who had just retired as a park ranger and lived in Carroll County, to jump into the race.

He was somewhat reluctant until the Sons of Confederate Veterans, based in Virginia, decided to provide financial backing for his campaign. The money they poured into his campaign provided an early edge, and then it all changed for Leroy Jefferson.

Libby Thomas decided she liked Leroy enough to throw her backing and wealth behind his campaign. She understood what the positive implications would be if an educated and qualified black man were elected sheriff. Carroll County was trying to develop a new persona, and it was hoping to attract new businesses and wealthy residents from out of state, those who might want not only to live in the Blue Ridge Mountains but also to stay close to populated areas in Virginia and North Carolina.

While the local pundits had predicted a close race, Leroy's campaign of honesty and integrity won over a clear majority of the voters. He smiled as he thought of all that and watched Laneisha sleeping in the hammock.

She was startled out of her sleep when Leroy's cell phone began to ring. He crossed the porch and picked his phone up from the wicker table. In a moment, he knew the county dispatcher was calling.

"This is Sheriff Jefferson," he answered.

"Well, heck yeah. I know this is you, Sheriff, 'cause I just called you!"

Leroy smiled as he recognized the voice. "Well, Josey Marshall, I know it can't be good if you are calling this time of the evening."

"Well, Sheriff, it ain't no good at all. Some ten minutes ago, we got a call that two bodies were lying in the alley behind the Pantry, on Court Street. Sue Ann Kollman is on duty and was just getting back to downtown. She got there in five minutes. Now, Sheriff, you will not believe what she found."

The sheriff winced. "Joey, spare me the drama. What did she find?"

"Well, Sheriff, she found Donnie Akers and Bobbie Joe Turner on the ground. Plumb dead in the alley."

Leroy immediately recognized both names as two local drug kingpins.

"And, Sheriff, it gets worse. These boys weren't shot or nothing. There were…now what is the word I'm lookin' for?

Got it! They were decapitated. That's right, Sheriff. Someone cut off their heads!"

For a moment, Leroy was speechless. "Have you called anyone else, Joey?"

"No, sir, just you."

"Good. I think Levi is on call tonight. Call him, and get him over there. Call the state police in Wytheville. Alert the duty officer and the folks in the crime lab. We are going to need some help on this one."

The sheriff hung up and looked at his wife, who was now wide awake from her nap. Laneisha looked at him and said, "I can just tell by the look on your face, Leroy Jefferson, that some shit just hit the fan."

Leroy walked over and gave her a kiss. "Well, right now I can tell you that our two most influential redneck drug dealers are dead. Kollman found them downtown. They were right behind the Deutsche Pantry. And whoever did it wanted to send a message. Two men in four parts."

Laneisha looked at him quizzically.

"Someone played the samurai tonight," said Leroy, "and chopped their heads off."

Laneisha was *speechless.*

CHAPTER 6

The lights on Estrada's Ford F-150 automatically came on as they turned off Highway 52 and onto Hanging Tree Road. Estrada looked in his rearview mirror and could not see anyone behind them. He knew Tony Esquivel and Luis Solis were not far behind, though. He watched Medina, who was sitting in the passenger seat, send a text message to them.

Within a few miles, they came to the metal bridge that crossed Big Reed Island Creek. Estrada punched a twelve-digit code into the keypad of the remote control in his hand. Within a few seconds, the metal gate started to lift and went straight up.

He drove across the narrow bridge and turned right on the other side of the creek. The road twisted and turned for a mile. It went through a narrow swath of tall pines and wild rhododendrons. Medina removed a second remote control and pushed the largest button. The ten-foot solid-metal gate started to swing open, and the lights illuminated the entry to the compound.

As soon as the front wheels touched the metal plates on the bridge, a dozen Rottweilers began to bark in their cages on the property. Estrada had the remote control to open the small gates that would release the dogs onto the property. All twelve dogs were trained to attack on command.

Estrada smiled after letting the truck roll to a stop in front of the first stall of the five-car garage. The entire complex covered about one hundred acres. Until Estrada purchased the property, it had been a Christmas tree farm. The owner had decided to retire and was pleased to sell the land to the wonderful Mexican couple that paid in cash.

Estrada admired how the creek provided a natural barrier to the property. The creek was too deep and rocky for any truck to cross; any motor vehicle had to use the bridge. He had spent over $1.5 million to renovate the main building for his family and to renovate the small house for Medina and his girlfriend. Both Solis and Esquivel, who were single, had their own small cabins.

The next two hundred thousand he had spent was on the state-of-the-art security system. All three nonriver sides of the property were covered by ten-foot-high fences, and electric mesh ran along the top of each fence line. He was confident that any attack on the compound would be delayed long enough for them to escape or to give them adequate time to prepare a deadly response.

After stepping out of his truck, he immediately heard the creek gate start to open when Esquivel and Solis approached. Estrada waited for the other two; Medina removed their weapons from the back seat of the truck. Estrada waved and signaled the other two to join them in the main house.

Inside, Estrada stood and gazed at his reflection in the full-length mirror in the foyer. He was covered in blood. His wife, Elva, walked toward him and stopped. "My God," she said, "I hope the other guy looks worse than you do! Shit, you are covered with blood. You are blessed a cop didn't stop you for something."

"My little *chavala*, the other guy don't look at nothing! His eyes stopped seeing when I chopped his head off! It was crazy! I felt like a Japanese samurai or something like that. But that shit is over. Those two motherfucker rednecks are dead."

Maria Medina got up from the table and walked to them. She looked at her husband, Medina. "What, no blood on you? Did you stay in the truck?"

Medina smiled. "Well, my sweetheart, I killed the other ten gringos with my pocketknife!"

All four started to howl, and Estrada stripped off his shirt and headed to the kitchen. He opened the refrigerator and took out two beers. He threw one to Medina and sat down at the table. The others quickly joined him.

"We all know what to expect now, don't we?" said Estrada. "We have cut off the heads of the two largest serpents. But we know snakes can live for some time without heads."

As he spoke, Esquivel and Solis came into the house and joined them at the table.

Medina looked at all of them and said, "We must act quickly to wipe out the bulk of their organization. By my estimate, nine of their lieutenants must be killed. So, we have twenty-two of our soldiers within one hundred miles of Carroll County, and we must use them to get the job done. And we must do it quickly.

"No doubt the local sheriff will get the state police and the DEA to help them on this. They will understand what is happening and will want to put an end to it."

"Amigo, I agree. Speed is of the essence!" Estrada said. "But we have another problem to deal with as well."

Medina shook his head. Elva threw up her hands and said, "What do you mean another problem?"

Estrada looked at her. "While we were in the alley, I saw someone watching us from the back of the restaurant. I couldn't see their faces, but I'm sure it was a woman and a little girl. The woman had a white cap on top of her head. She also wore a long skirt."

Elva piped in and said, "So, were you behind the Pantry?"

Estrada nodded. "I think we can be sure she is a Mennonite, and she probably works at the restaurant. And the little girl is probably hers."

Maria looked at her husband, Medina. "Listen, you two, all those Mennonites are a pretty tight group. They have a bakery on Highway Fifty-Eight, and they all go to their church in Hillsville. I don't think there are too many of them."

Estrada looked at them all. "I don't worry about all of them. Only the woman and little girl who saw Roger, Tony, Luis, and me. They could get us in big trouble. I need to wash up before we eat. Then we can work on a plan to find this woman before the cops do."

Maria looked at him. "What will you do with this woman and her child when you find them?"

Estrada stood and leaned in her direction. "I will help them find *their Mennonite heaven*!"

CHAPTER 7

Sheriff Jefferson pulled up to the area behind the Deutsche Pantry and parked near several other deputies who had already arrived. He saw Dr. Kahn, the Carroll County coroner, standing alongside Levi Blackburn, the senior investigator with the sheriff's department.

Just as he got out of his car, Jim Craig—the lead investigator from the Virginia State Police district office in Wytheville—pulled in beside him. He nodded at the sheriff as he raised his cell phone to his ear.

Levi walked over to the sheriff and said, "This makes my day. Two idiots get their heads chopped off, and now I have to listen to the biggest asshole cop in Southwest Virginia! I thought Craig was supposed to be retired by now."

The sheriff put his arm around Levi's shoulder. "Now, Levi, I expect you to be nice to Jim and to do what you can to work with him on this. I know there is bad blood between you two, but do what you need to do to put it behind you."

Levi rolled his eyes as he led the sheriff to the crime scene. Two bodies were lying prone on the pavement. Bloody white sheets covered them. Dr. Kahn walked over to the sheriff.

"Well, Doc, what do we have here?" the sheriff asked.

"Well, Leroy, this is pretty straightforward. These two were stabbed at least twenty times. That is the cause of death. Then, for good measure, someone chopped off their heads. Probably used a butcher knife, I suspect."

Levi looked at the nearby buildings. "Not one camera on this side of the street. Plenty around the corner covering the government center, but there's not one in this alley. Whoever did this planned it real well."

Jim Craig approached the group as Levi was speaking. "Now, Blackburn, it doesn't take a rocket scientist to figure out who was responsible for this. Since Bobby Joe Turner and Donnie Akers headed your local drug enterprise, I believe it might be safe to assume your Latino cartel brothers had something to do with it."

Levi seethed. "What a brilliant deduction, Watson! You get the prize for stating the obvious. Duh. I mean really, Craig, did you have to drive all the way from Wytheville to tell us that?"

The sheriff smiled. "All right, you two. Who is going to call Jeannie Wishart at the DEA office?"

"I know Jeannie fairly well. I will call her," said Craig.

Levi snickered. "You wish you knew her well! *Dream on*!"

CHAPTER 8

The mood in the deli went from somber to normal after Libby's departure. Quinn and Louisa sat for a while after they finished eating. Louisa reached over, took Quinn's hands in hers, and smiled. "Oh, Quinn, you just make me feel good all over—you big hunk. I don't care a bit if my horse missed winning all the Triple Crown stuff. I would give it all up just to snuggle in your arms!"

Quinn kicked her under the table. "Jeez, Louisa, give the woman a break. The most important thing in her life slipped away from her in a mere second or two. And to make matters worse, the whole freaking world was watching. I know you don't like her one bit, but every person deserves a little slack. Most folks don't have a clue about all the good she has done here in Carroll County and Grayson County. The drug and alcohol rehab center and the shelter for battered women wouldn't exist without her philanthropy."

Louisa frowned. "McSpain, I can't dispute any of that. But listen, big fella, that woman has the most inflated ego in all of Southwest Virginia. She crushes business associates who get in her way. Sure, she might have a tiny bit of compassion, but she is truly rotten to the core! She must be related to your best friend—the Donald! Oh, I almost forgot something. Sharon, would you mind coming over here with a mop? Libby wet herself just sittin' next to ole Quinn here. The floor is dangerously slippery."

Sharon came out of the kitchen and looked at them both; they were bent over in laughter. "Now, Louisa, you had better keep an eye on your man 'cause we all know Libby gets what she has her eye on. And she sure 'nuff did have her eyes on all of ole Quinn!"

Quinn stood and took Louisa's hand. "Now, Sharon, as you are my witness, my heart has only enough room for one woman. Now, if this one ever kicks me to the ditch, I do believe I will need a reserved seat in this here deli!"

With that, he raced to the door with Louisa in hot pursuit. He opened the driver's side door of his truck and dived in. Within the next moment, Louisa jumped in and snuggled beside him. She leaned in and held the lower part of his earlobe in her teeth. Quinn tried not to move until he felt her hand start to unbuckle his belt. Soon he was moaning.

She loosened her teeth's grip on his ear. "Well, big man, two very attractive women took off all your clothes and ogled you in there. Now, I know it's four miles to the house from here."

Quinn smiled. "Get in your car, and follow me home before I—"

Louisa put a finger on his lips. "I am going to stop at the Dollar General to pick up a few things. Promise you won't cool off before I get home."

Quinn started his truck and watched her slide into her Volvo. He looked in the rearview mirror as he backed out. A second earlier, he would have seen a Harley fly out of the deli parking lot and head straight to the Blue Ridge Parkway.

Neither saw the Harley.

Tommie Cruz knew exactly where he was going. He had practiced these moves on many occasions. The difference now was that this was his moment of truth. He drove for two miles, and then he slowed as he turned off the parkway and onto the dirt-access cutoff to State Road 608, which paralleled the parkway.

He stopped his motorcycle in a thick clump of pines. He was not ten feet from the parkway pavement and no more than ten feet from the oncoming traffic. He threw the kickstand out, reached into his saddlebag, and pulled out his Taurus .44 Magnum. The scope was in place. He quickly braced himself on the trunk of a pine tree and aimed straight at the cars coming on the Parkway toward him.

He didn't have to wait long before he saw Quinn's Dodge Ram coming down the road. He was not a half mile away. As he applied pressure to the trigger, he heard a strange sound coming from the tall grass he was standing in.

He took his eye off the approaching truck and looked at the copperhead coiled some three feet from his boot. He started to squeeze the trigger as he returned his gaze to the truck. Instinctively he squeezed the trigger, and the round left the chamber.

Without a moment's thought, he threw the pistol back in the saddlebag, picked up the empty casing, threw his leg over the Harley, and started it. He twisted the throttle, causing the Harley to roar, and soon he was flying down Highway 608 and heading back to Fancy Gap. In his mind's eye, he still saw the snake, and he knew it had affected his shot.

While he was sure he had hit the windshield, he didn't know if his intended target had been hit. He also knew he couldn't hang around to find out.

Quinn took his eyes off the parkway for a second, and he looked at the side of the road. Before he could look at the road again, he felt the impact of the windshield and the rear window shattering. He felt the pieces of glass hitting all corners of the cab.

He blinked and realized his sunglasses had protected his eyes. Quinn floored the gas pedal, accelerating his truck. He kept it that way until he reached the parkway's next turnoff.

The truck slid when he smashed the brake pedal. The tires screeched until the truck came to a stop. Quinn opened the center console and wrapped his hand around his Smith & Wesson Governor. He opened his door and jumped onto the grass.

Quinn ran on the side of Highway 608, toward the spot where the windshield had shattered. He soon arrived at the crossover to the 608. He stopped and listened. Everything was quiet until a car coming down the Blue Ridge Parkway slammed on its brakes and skidded to a stop.

Louisa jumped out of her Volvo and ran to the spot in the bushes. A frightened look was on her face. "Jesus, Quinn, what the hell just happened?"

Quinn looked up at her. "Well, I know what just happened. I just don't know why."

She looked him over, from head to toe. "Are you OK? You've got blood on your shirt. Were you hit?"

Quinn took her in his arms. "Nah, it was close, but the shooter just missed."

After a moment, he let her go, and they walked a few steps away.

Louisa abruptly stopped and pointed down to where the grass met the pavement. "Look at that, McSpain. Seems like whoever took that shot at you was driving on two wheels and took off in a hurry. The rear wheel spun when it hit the pavement."

Quinn crouched down and took some dirt that had been thrown onto the pavement. "By the size of this track, it was a large bike. Probably a Harley, and whoever it was didn't waste any time getting out of here. The shooter had a plan and kept to it. Didn't need to wait to see if I was hit or not."

"Look at me, Quinn. I think you were plumb lucky you had your sunglasses on. You've got minor cuts on your forehead and cheeks."

He took her head in his hands and turned it from side to side. "Well, I'm blessed you weren't with me."

She hugged him, and he reached for his cell phone. He said, "Just when I expected our lives to be nice and peaceful, some idiot tries to kill me. That's crazy. OK, guess we better call our new sheriff and pass along the good news."

Louisa looked away for a moment. "We had better notify the park ranger since you were on federal property when the attack occurred. I bet the shooter was on the county road when the shot was taken, though."

Quinn speed-dialed a number on his phone.

"So, for the grace of God," said the sheriff, "why do I have the pleasure of Quinn McSpain on the other end of this call?"

"Well, Sheriff, I need to ask if you have been doing target practice on the Blue Ridge Parkway this afternoon. Now, my friend, before you answer that, I think I already know the answer. Since the shot that just came through my front windshield didn't kill me, I know it couldn't have been you."

A pause followed, which Quinn had expected.

"Listen, Quinn, I hope you are joking. Are you saying someone just took a shot at you? I really do hope that isn't the case."

"Well, Leroy Jefferson, that's exactly what happened. At about mile marker one ninety-seven on the Parkway, at the Highway Six Hundred Eight crossover. Bullet went right through the middle of the windshield and out the back window. And, not to worry. Other than a few cuts on my face, I'm OK."

"Thank God for that! Listen, I am going to leave the office, and I'll be there in ten minutes. I'll get Levi to meet us there as well. Now, your incident is crazy. First there was what happened last night and now this."

"I'm almost frightened to ask what happened last night," Quinn said.

"Well, if you don't hear about it from me, you will read about it in the newspaper. Seems as if two of our top local redneck drug lords lost their heads last night. We found them in the alley behind the Deutsche Pantry, on Court Street.

"Whoever killed them intended to send a message because they didn't shoot them. They chopped their heads off. Never seen anything like it before. But, hey, that was last night, and now I have a bigger problem. Not good to have someone try to kill my best friend. You two should keep your heads low till I get out there. You don't think it could have been Libby, do you?" he said, and then he hung up.

Quinn looked at Louisa *and smiled.*

CHAPTER 9

Hope Showalter trembled as she drove from the Pantry. Her mind rolled through the horrific scene she had just witnessed. She looked at Hannah, who was buckled in and looked straight ahead. The fact they had witnessed two men being beheaded was almost impossible to process.

She was halfway to Volunteer Gap before she turned around and headed in another direction. She knew she needed to share what they had just seen with someone. She drove on autopilot, and her mind raced in a million directions.

Before she knew it, she had driven into a familiar driveway; its motion light came on, and she stopped her old van and cut off the engine. She didn't move for several minutes. Then the porch light came on, and a familiar figure walked onto the porch.

Pastor Frank Kauffmann recognized Hope's van but was surprised to see it in his driveway at that time of night. He and his wife, Stella, had spent hours counseling Hope after her husband passed on. They were quite fond of Hope and Hannah.

He and his wife had been at the church and school for the past five years. Since they were nearing retirement age, he had left a much larger church he was heading in Canada to work with a much smaller congregation and to be in a much milder climate.

He walked down the porch stairs and to the driver's side window. Hope stared straight ahead before she realized he was standing there. "Oh my God, Frank, you scared me," she muttered, and she swung her door open.

Hannah jumped out of the passenger seat and ran up the stairs. Crying, she jumped into Stella Kauffmann's arms, who was now standing in the middle of the porch. She turned and walked into the house. Hope and Frank were close behind.

Within a moment, they were all seated at the kitchen table. Stella looked at Hope and Hannah with a concerned look in her eyes. "My God, Hope, what have you two been through tonight?"

Hope began to sob uncontrollably. No one spoke until she whispered, "We witnessed a savage murder tonight! My God, I could not move when I saw what was happening right before our eyes. The brutality of it hasn't sunk in yet."

Stella reached over and took both of her hands. "Tell us what happened, my child."

Through her tears, Hope said, "My eyes witnessed savagery at its worst, but my soul refused to see what was happening before my eyes. I have read of such things happening in faraway places, or I've seen them on television. Some thirty feet from where we stood silently, merciless savages killed two men. The two men were stabbed several times, but the violence didn't end there. One man used a butcher knife to chop off their heads.

"He simply smiled after he finished. Then he looked up and saw us standing on the back porch of the Pantry. We were frozen in fear; he was frozen while digesting the fact we were there. In a moment, he and the other man started toward us.

"I took Hannah, and we ran in through the back door and locked it behind us. We stopped short of the front door when we saw a sheriff's car drive past the entrance slowly. Whoever was driving could not see us since the Pantry lights were out.

"I looked through the side window and saw the killers stop when they saw the deputy's car. They turned and went back to their trucks. Hannah and I waited for some time—until we were sure they had gone. We started to drive back to our house in Volunteer Gap, and I decided I needed to tell someone about what we had witnessed. I have never been so frightened in my life!"

After a moment, Pastor Frank leaned over and hugged her. "Hope, you did the right thing by coming here. Do you think they might have seen you drive away?"

"No, they were long gone when we left. I'm sure of it. But there is no doubt they know we saw them kill those men in cold blood. And one of them got a good look at us. Listen, Frank, this is crazy! Won't those men stop at nothing to kill us?"

"My dearest Hope, we can pray for the souls of the men who were murdered tonight. We then must do whatever it takes to protect you and Hannah from whatever harm might come your way. We are a strong and resilient Mennonite community here in Hillsville. We will come together to protect you both in whatever ways we can!"

Hope wiped the tears from her eyes. "Pastor Frank, our lives are in your hands and *God's will.*"

CHAPTER 10

Tommie Cruz drove his motorcycle north on Highway 52. When he reached the Hillsville bypass, he headed back to Galax. He fumed because he might not have killed McSpain with his single shot. In his mind's eye, he kept seeing the window shattering; in his mind's eye, he kept searching for details that would indicate whether the man had been hit.

He took his time driving back along Highway 58. He knew the Virginia State Police loved to set up at the bottoms of the many hills along that stretch of highway and to ticket drivers who exceeded the speed limit. He cautiously followed the speed limit, which was thirty-five miles per hour once he entered Galax's city limits.

Once in the alleyway behind his building, he quickly parked his Harley and locked the doors behind him. Once inside, he decided he needed to deal with the sudden urge to down a beer.

Within a few steps, he unlocked the front door and walked down the steps to Main Street, which he crossed before entering Macado's. This was the closest bar, and it had a decent restaurant as well. He pulled up a stool at the end of the bar, which was relatively empty.

Jake, the bartender, watched Tommie in the mirror and turned as he sat. “Well, to what do I owe the honor of having the smartest and best-looking man in all of Galax sitting in front of me?”

Tommie smiled. “Jake, it’s your lucky day. I’m thirsty, and I’ve got enough change in my pocket to buy a few.”

Jake smiled because he believed Tommie was flush with money; the man always bought the best beers, always left large tips, and always paid in cash. He just didn’t know what his last name was. “The regular, Tommie, or something new?”

Tommie frowned. “I think I need a Stella today. I was thinking of a Heineken, but I want a Stella.”

Jake took a chilled glass from the cooler and started to pour a pint. After he topped off the beer with the right amount of foam, he turned and placed the glass on a coaster in front of Tommie. “Cheers, my friend. Enjoy. I hope your day went well.”

Tommie took a long first sip. “Jake, my day sucked. I had a plan that needed to come to life today, but I failed miserably. Failure doesn’t happen very often in my life. Today, though, it just didn’t go the way I had planned. I fucked the pooch.”

“Damn, Tommie, sorry ’bout that. I know you like to get your shit right the first time in whatever you do. Sucks, my friend. But, hell, tomorrow is another day, and you might just get another chance.”

Jake watched Tommie’s expression tighten.

"Oh," said Tommie, "you can take that to the bank. I will try again, and I will succeed!"

Jake was surprised that this normally even-tempered person had his dander up.

Before either spoke again, a voice rang out after the door to the bar opened and closed. Tommie looked at the mirror behind the bar and saw a woman approaching him.

"Must be my lucky day to have my favorite neighbor sitting at the bar," she said.

Tommie recognized the female voice. Missy was the young woman who rented an apartment in the building next to his. She worked in the local hardware store, and most people found her very attractive. Tommie had watched her sunbathing in the nude on the rooftop next door. He felt a certain attraction to her, yet he knew any personal relationship was risky.

She had the reputation of being a tease with local men, whether they were single or married and whether they were attempting to win her attention or not. She did not discriminate. The word on the street in Galax, however, was that Missy was not in any hurry to start any relationships. Some were convinced she wanted nothing to do with any of the local talent.

He caught himself staring at her ample breasts, which were barely held in her skimpy halter top. Missy was on the short side, but she had tight and muscular legs, along with a very small waistline. Her short shorts highlighted her tanned legs.

Missy smiled at Tommie as she slid onto the barstool next to his. "I know you like what you see, Tommie. I think it's time you give in a little to temptation; let me show you what you're missing."

Tommie looked straight ahead. "Missy, what I'm looking at is my empty glass. I need to decide if I'm going to have another one or not. I've had a rotten day, so I think I deserve another beer."

Missy put her thumb on his chin and turned his head in her direction. "Let me suggest that I can help you with all that. Let's walk over to the hardware store and get us a couple of bottles of chilled Chardonnay at the wine shop next door. We can take those two bottles and our little ole selves up to my rooftop, and we can enjoy the last few hours of glorious sunshine this afternoon. I can give you a nice massage that will make you forget all that shit that is bothering you right now."

Tommie felt her hand inching up his leg, and he felt a very positive response in his groin. He looked up and saw Jake, who was within earshot. He was smiling at him. "That will be five bucks for the Stella, Tommie."

Missy reached into her pocket, took out a five-dollar bill, and threw it on the bar. "My treat, Tommie, but you gotta spring for the wine."

They both stood and turned toward the door. Jake took the five-dollar bill and smiled. "You two have a great rest of the afternoon!"

As soon as the door slammed shut, he thought, I really do need to find out what *his last name is.*

☆ ☆ ☆

Sheriff Jefferson drove through the curves on Highway 608 and slowed as he approached the parkway access road. The thought of someone attempting to kill his best friend was disturbing. He parked near Quinn's truck, which was in a grassy spot between the highway and the parkway. Quinn and Louisa were talking with Billy Sykes, the local park ranger who had parked on the side of the parkway.

"I declare, McSpain," said Leroy, "if you wanted some air in the big ole Ram, I think you might have rolled the windows down. Or at least turned on the air conditioner!"

Louisa laughed as she hugged Leroy. "You're right, Leroy. The man does have a flair for the dramatic. To think he needed to have someone shoot out the windshield just to get a bit more air in the truck is, well…so him!"

All four of them were laughing.

"This is crazy, Quinn!" said Leroy. "Why, in God's name, would anyone take a shot at you? You have killed off or incarcerated about any miscreant who might want you dead."

Quinn held up his right hand and pointed at Louisa. "Don't be sure it's me someone is after. Think about it: after all those years in the FBI and now with all the shit she has stirred up in these hills. Could there be any doubt?"

Leroy shook his head. "Well, Billy, what do you think about all this?"

The park ranger walked toward the bushes nearest to the state road. "Sheriff, looks to me as if the shooter was parked right here on county property when the shot was taken. The two tire marks in the grass indicate he or she was driving a large motorcycle. From what I see, I don't think this was a random shooting by some crazy person. No, indeed. I believe the shooter intended for Quinn to be the target.

"If someone just wanted to shoot at anyone on the parkway, there are far better places to choose than this. My theory is that whoever took the shot knew Quinn was going to turn off the parkway in another mile or so. I am certain this was premeditated and planned to the *n*th degree. Since the shooter was so close to the parkway, I suggest that something went wrong just before he or she pulled the trigger. The shooter also knew that only one shot could be taken."

Quinn smiled. "Brilliant deductive reasoning, my friend, and I agree with you completely. The shooter knew what he or she was doing. Chose the spot and took the single shot. Then the plan was finished. By now, however, the shooter probably knows the shot barely missed and that the prize has yet to be attained."

Leroy said, "I will have our deputies talk with the folks who live along Highway Six Hundred Eight. They can see if anyone saw or heard a motorcycle in the area at the time. I'll have them check the other side of the parkway for the slug."

Louisa smirked. "OK, I buy all that. No witnesses and probably no evidence. What that leaves me with is simply one conclusion: whoever the bitch is, he or she will probably *try again.*"

☆ ☆ ☆

It was only two blocks to the wine shop from Macado's. Tommie held the door open for Missy, and she brushed against him as she entered. He saw Karen Boyd behind the counter. She was looking at both of them walk in.

Karen owned both the wine shop and the connected hardware store. She respected Missy, both for being a great employee and for putting herself through graduate school. She took online classes at Virginia Tech at night and on weekends. Karen also knew Missy had a crush on Tommie. "Well, now," said Karen, "look who decided to grace me with their presence. My favorite manager and the mysterious man she is infatuated with."

Missy blushed. "Now, Karen, the truth is I just picked this guy up on the street."

Karen smiled. "Well, you're already having a better day than I am. My computer went on the fritz when I tried to upload Windows Ten. A complete disaster! I just hope I didn't lose too many important files."

Tommie looked at her. "Well, if little ole me can help little ole you, can I get paid in wine today?"

"Are you serious, Tommie? If you are and you can fix it, you can have the pick of the wine litter. So, just follow me to my office, and we'll see what you think."

He followed Karen, and Missy was right behind him. After Karen unlocked the opening screen, he sat down and looked at the laptop in front of him. In a moment, he began typing as fast as either woman had seen a person type.

Missy and Karen were mesmerized as screenshot after screenshot flew by. Within five minutes, he stopped, powered the laptop down, and restarted it. He stood when the screen came to life. He looked at Karen. "You may now sit and enjoy the new Windows Ten."

She slowly sat in the chair and started to explore what she was looking at. "Oh my God. This is wonderful!" she exclaimed as she started typing.

Tommie slipped out of the office with Missy in hand. He stopped at the refrigerated wine chest and took out a Chardonnay and a pinot grigio. He held them up to Missy, who nodded approval.

His next stop was the rack that held the expensive reds. After a moment, he slid out the bottle he wanted.

"What kind is that?" Missy asked.

Tommie held up the bottle. "Elizabeth Spencer Cabernet Sauvignon. Exquisite! One of my favorites."

Missy took it from him and fondled it up against her breasts. "I already know I'm going to love this one," she said seductively.

Karen was still in her office. She was fixated on her now-functioning laptop, and she never saw them leave the store.

Tommie held Missy's hand as they crossed the street to the front door of her apartment. She unlocked the door, smiled as they walked in, and locked the door behind them. Tommie looked around and said, "This is a real nice place. Doesn't Karen own this building?"

"She does," replied Missy, opening her bedroom door. "Now, be a good boy. Open the wine for us while I get my bikini on."

It was Tommie's time to smile, and he headed to the kitchen. He quickly found the corkscrew and two wineglasses. He was impressed with how clean and orderly the kitchen was. As he poured the white wine, Missy came into the kitchen.

Tommie couldn't help but notice how her tiny bikini just barely contained her ample curves. He took two glasses of wine and walked to her; he offered her one, which she accepted. She held it between two fingers and smiled. Before he could say anything, she said, "Now, you gotta tell me, handsome, how in the world did you fix Karen's computer so damn quickly? That was impressive!"

He took his wineglass and clinked it with hers. "Missy, I'm a man of many talents. I can take computers apart and put them back together blindfolded. I can write complex programs to run just about anything."

"So, exactly where did you learn all this interesting and useful shit?" she asked.

He put his finger to his lips. "For me to know and for you to find out. Maybe."

Before she could answer, he took her hand and led her to the inner stairwell that led to the roof. Once at the top, she twisted the knob lock open, and they stepped onto the roof. She led him to the area she had set up to sunbathe.

The raised deck was the size of a king-size bed. Missy took several of the pillows strewn about and set up a sitting area for both of them.

Tommie set the wine cooler down and removed the open bottle of white wine. He filled their glasses, and Missy walked over to the nearby table. She picked up a bottle of dark suntan oil. When she came back, she sat in his lap.

She took a sip of wine and set her glass down. Her right hand reached around her back, and she slowly undid the knot holding the strings together. The top fell to her lap.

He saw that her breasts were as tan as the rest of her torso. He also felt an immediate reaction. Blood rushed to his manhood. Without hesitation, he stood and slipped off his cotton shorts.

Missy sat back against a pillow and admired his manhood. He was endowed well beyond what was considered normal. She stood, still taking it all in, and she walked over to the wine bottle.

She took hold of the bottle in one hand and a handful of ice in the other. When she returned, she poured more wine in his glass and slowly cupped his jewels in the ice.

Tommie never fidgeted—not even the slightest twitch. He only sipped his wine calmly. “Do you like this Chardonnay?” he asked her.

Before she answered, she slid her hand with the ice away from him and rubbed her lips with two of the cubes. “It’s very nice. I like the buttery taste of it and the fact it isn’t too oaky. But don’t get me wrong. What I really like is that piece of oak you brought to the party. Now, I must tell you something. By choice, I haven’t been with a man in quite some time,” said Missy, and she smiled.

Tommie groaned as the ice in her hand began to melt. Missy slowly sat back on the bench and pulled Tommie in her direction. She slipped down beneath him until his manhood was set firmly between her ample breasts. He slowly and rhythmically slid back and forth as she melted ice over his excitement.

Her interest grew as he worked his way down her body. Eventually, he licked her nipples. She began to writhe with passion. Her desire to be taken grew. He teased her unmercifully as he rubbed every inch of flesh between her legs but just gave her hints of immediate pleasure.

Missy wrapped her hands behind his neck and locked her fingers. He slowly entered her with small thrusts, exciting her to no end. Her whole body tingled, and she felt every bit of his manhood inside her. She responded to his movements, tightening her inner self to heighten her pleasure.

They became one as they unleashed their lust on each other; time was lost on them both. Missy recoiled with orgasm after orgasm. She bit his ear, and she moaned, "God, I never want this to end!"

Tommie controlled himself, and he smiled as he massaged his droplets of sweat into her breasts. "Girl, this is your lucky day 'cause *I'm taking you to new places*!"

CHAPTER 11

Roger Medina tucked his 9 mm into his belt holster because he knew Estrada was getting ready to leave the compound. He walked to the front window in the living room and looked out. He snarled as he saw the wisps of white smoke coming up through the trees on the hillside in front of the compound.

He knew the granny witch lived on top of the mountain he was looking at. He was taken with the notion that this old woman possessed magical powers he didn't understand.

As Estrada entered the room, he looked at Medina and said, "What are you growling at?"

"Look at the smoke coming out of the trees. You know that old, crazy mountain witch is there watching us. I want to kill that old bitch!"

What Medina was referring to was the granny witch who lived high on the hill across the river from the compound. Granny "Tiller"—as she was known to those in Carroll County who were old enough to have seen her—was a frightful legend in those parts.

Tiller was thought to be a descendent of the original Appalachian queens, who were daughters of the Celts and the offspring of Druids. All were medieval mavens and natives of the old-world craft. Many believed Tiller still had Celt and Cherokee magic in her bones.

Estrada's wife, Elva, entered the room and saw both men staring out the window. As soon as she joined them, she saw the smoke as well. Everyone in the compound knew Elva was superstitious, and everyone knew she was the only one of them to have ever set eyes on Tiller.

When her pet Chihuahua had taken ill and had not been given any chance to live by the local vet, Elva took the sick dog through the woods and up the mountain, and she left it on Tiller's front porch. Ten days later, Tiller came down the mountain and crossed the river to the edge of the compound.

Elva saw her when she crossed the river. She opened the main gate and rushed to the entrance. As she arrived, Tiller let the dog down, and he ran toward Elva with his tail wagging happily. Tiller offered the slightest smile before turning and heading back to the river.

Elva's family was shocked at the dog's new and improved state of health. The story was not lost on Estrada. He always harbored some fear of superstitious things and people. Whatever Tiller had done was not lost on him. He found new respect and fear of these magic women—these healers of wounds and tellers of fortunes and casters of hexes.

Medina was about to speak when Elva put her finger to his lips. "I know what you are thinking. I know you think she has returned because you see the smoke. Do not ever think of doing anything to that woman. She is more powerful than you or any of us. You stay away from that witch!"

Estrada took her hand. "Elva, not to worry. None of us will harm that crazy woman. I believe there is old blood in her veins; she has a power we do not understand. If I killed her, I would only kill the flesh. And I don't need her dark spirit haunting me all the way to hell."

Medina rolled his eyes, and he thought, Fuck that old blood. I will kill that witch someday and send her to *Beulah land*!

* * *

The sunlight broke over the eastern ridge and painted the western slope of the next ridge. Louisa caught a glimpse of the ridge as she rolled over to look at the horizon. This was, by far, her favorite part of the day: when she could take as long as she wanted to absorb the early morning light.

The years she lived and worked in the District of Columbia had faded in her memory; they had become just another blip on the massive radar screen of humanity. She embraced the peace and tranquility she had found in Southwest Virginia.

She heard the floor creak as Quinn tiptoed into the bedroom. She slowly turned and saw him standing in front of her. He was holding two cups of steaming coffee. "So," she said, "I get curb service this morning, even though you were the one to barely escape death yesterday."

Quinn smiled and sat on the edge of the bed. He set her cup on her nightstand. "Oh, did something happen yesterday that I forgot about?" Quinn said, smirking.

"Let me tell you what I think, McSpain. I think your girlfriend, Libby, hired a hit man to take me out of the picture." She reached for her coffee. "I saw the way she looked at you in the deli before she left. I'll bet she would forget all about her little filly losing the Triple Crown if she could corral your ole butt. She just didn't know I wasn't in the truck."

Quinn took a long sip from his coffee before he replied. "My dearest, neither these eyes nor my heart has interest in any other person than little ole you. Sure, Libby is beautiful, wealthy, and a tad sexy, but that woman couldn't find a square inch of space in my little ole heart. You got it all locked up."

Louisa set her cup down and worked her way to the corner of the bed he was sitting on. "OK. I agree it probably wasn't Libby, but then who? Frankly I thought you were done being a target of demented criminals and people who hated you enough to try to kill you. So, big man, as I gazed at these beautiful ridges this morning, I gave all that some uncomplicated thought."

Quinn cocked his head a bit after her comment.

"Don't look so inquisitive. I'm gonna tell you what I think is happening. In the several years or so we have cohabitated here in this paradise we call home, we have been involved in two messy situations—through no fault of our own.

"One sick and demented Catholic priest is dead, and several international terrorists are dead. That's because we helped track them down and sped up their ultimate demises. Don't get me wrong. I'm happy as a pig in shit that all that came to pass. And the worst that happened to…well, me…is that I got shot.

"I haven't heard from any of my former FBI colleagues about any dipshit who might have threatened to track us down in our retired lives and kill us. So, all of that put together in a cauldron of crap and stirred around means we are dealing with a local problem child who wants you or us dead.

"Of course, that leaves you, my baby boomer love object. But, then again, from your less-than-remarkable corporate career, I can hardly imagine that any of those corporate idiots you put in jail would have the balls to come after you."

As she finished, Louisa threw off the bedcovers, which reminded Quinn that she slept in the nude. He noticed that the twinkle in her eye was sending strong signals. "OK, Cleopatra. Back away," he said. "You got me thinking of who might desire to rid me of this no-rent-paying ex-government hack who has put my life in mortal danger!"

Louisa giggled as she grabbed a pillow and sat back against the headboard with her legs crossed.

"Now, that's more like it," said Quinn. He drank more coffee. "So, most of the corporate screw-ups I dealt with are in jail or retired, and I really can't think of anyone in that bunch who would have the moxie to come after me. Nah. I have to agree with you and surmise that the threat we are facing is home grown. I'm probably eighty percent sure of that."

When he stopped talking, he looked at Louisa. She was glowing as she tossed the pillow she had been hugging to the floor. She slowly spread her legs and dipped two fingers into her coffee cup. She stirred the coffee, removed her fingers, and began to gently massage her lips with her wet fingers.

Quinn quickly became aware of the stirring in his groin. Louisa noticed it as well. She got on her knees and said, "Time you got closer to your barista. Let's see if we can get a tall or a grande or my favorite—the venti—to play with."

In a moment, he tossed off his T-shirt, stripped off his jeans, took the coffee cup from her hands, and put it on the nightstand. "And I thought I was in trouble 'cause I was shot at yesterday. But you…just hope you survive the next hour or so, girlfriend!"

"Bring it on, McSpain. *Just bring it on.*"

☆ ☆ ☆

A week had passed since the killings at the Pantry. Estrada and Medina could not wait any longer. They needed to try to find the woman and child, the only people who had witnessed the murders of Akers and Turner. Estrada decided they needed to have lunch at the Pantry to see if they recognized any of the Mennonite women and young girls working there.

Estrada parked his truck right in front of the Pantry, on Court Street. He decided that going in at the busiest time of day might be the best time to blend in with the customers and to take a hard look at all the employees.

There was a long line at the order counter when they entered. Hope Showalter was in the tiny back office and did not see them enter. They placed their orders and sat at a middle table near the center of the Pantry. They looked at the four Mennonite women standing in the kitchen area. They also watched the younger women who brought the orders to the customers' tables.

Some ten minutes elapsed before their orders arrived. The waitress, a young woman, smiled at them as she set down the tray and placed their food in front of them. Medina smiled as she left, looked at Estrada, and said, "Jesus, they all look alike. Must be inbreeding. They all look like cousins!"

Estrada offered a tepid smile. "Listen, I don't recognize any of these women. I know it was starting to get dark, but I won't ever forget the face of that woman and the little girl."

As the young woman who delivered their food came by again, Estrada put up his hand. "Excuse me, young lady, but I'm curious about something. Are there more ladies who work here who are not here today?"

She stood there for a moment before responding. "Well, I think there are at least twenty of us who work here, but we all work at different times. Does that help you?"

"Yes, it does," he replied. "Thank you very much."

Medina looked perplexed. "So, Duke, what do we do now? I mean, we can't hang around this place."

Estrada took the last bite of his sandwich and looked at Medina. "We will visit their church, my friend, and see them all together."

"Wow. Great idea, boss, but…well, won't they notice us? I mean, two Mexican dudes in a room full of white people who all look like cousins. Shit, we might stand out!"

Just as he finished that sentence, Hope Showalter came out of her office. She stopped dead in her tracks when she looked to the middle of the Pantry and saw Estrada and Medina. She quickly pivoted and slipped back into the office.

Her hands quivered as she closed the door behind her. She recognized the killers and knew why they were at the Pantry. She waited a full ten minutes before she cracked the door open and looked to the center of the restaurant. The table was empty.

She walked out and asked who had delivered the food to the center table. One of the younger girls spun around. "I did, Hope, and they sure left a nice tip for me."

Hope took her into the office. "Did they say anything to you?"

"They sure did. They asked how many of us worked here. But that was all they asked."

"Thank you, sweetie; that is very helpful. You can go back to the kitchen now."

Hope sat at her desk and put her face in her hands. She knew she was frightened to her core. The killers were now hunting her, and Hillsville was a small area for them to cover. She knew her life and Hannah's life was in mortal danger.

After she composed herself, she went back into the kitchen. No more than five minutes had gone by when the front door opened and in walked Sheriff Jefferson. He lunched at the Pantry at least twice a week, and he always waved to Hope when he stopped by.

When his order was ready, Hope personally took the tray to the table where he was sitting. He smiled as she approached and said, "Now, you're making me feel real special, Hope Showalter. The manager herself is delivering my order."

Hope blushed as she set down the tray. "Do you mind if I sit for a moment, Sheriff?"

"Of course not, Hope. Please, sit down."

Once seated, Hope looked at him and asked, "Sheriff, has there been progress made on the terrible murders that happened in the alley? You have to understand that the staff is a bit fearful about coming to work and walking in the alley."

Leroy took a sip of sweet tea before he replied. "Hope, while the act that took place in the alley was horrific and barbaric, the killers were very specific in whom they targeted. It was a drug cartel doing its best to kill off the competition. I know that doesn't sound very reassuring, but there was nothing random about those murders. That was not good news for the victims, but it is good for all of us. I say this because the killers have no intentions of bothering us. We will never be on their radar screens.

"Truth be told, Hope, I'm so pleased that no one was here when that all happened. There is no telling what those killers might do to someone who had seen them."

Hope blanched as she listened to the sheriff's words. Leroy could tell she was affected by what he had said. "Hope, are you OK?"

She sat still for the longest moment and was deep in thought. Finally, she cleared her throat and said, "Sheriff, I'm fine. I just need time to sort out a few things on my mind." With that, she stood and took the sheriff's hand. "Thank you, and I enjoyed talking with you. Give my best to your lovely wife."

Leroy held her hand for a moment longer. "Hope, is there something you want to talk about?"

"No, Sheriff, there isn't. *At least for right now.*"

CHAPTER 12

Leroy Jefferson sat back in his chair and glanced at the clock on the side of his desk. He had been in his office since six thirty in the morning. He was reviewing all the information he had on the double homicides in the alley, as well as what little was known about the shots fired at Quinn.

He had invited several members of state and federal law enforcement agencies to meet with him at 9:00 a.m. in his conference room. At five to nine, Levi Blackburn knocked on his door and let himself in. "Sheriff, all the players have arrived, but are you sure we need that knucklehead Jim Craig here?"

Leroy smiled. "Levi, I know I can count on you to behave this morning. You know that Craig has lots of contacts all over Southwest Virginia—in the narcotics trafficking area. Contacts we could never possibly know."

"Dang, Leroy, I'll try my best to be nice to him, but you know...I just can't stomach his sorry ass."

"Well, Levi, just keep your eyes on Jeannie Wishart. She is smart and very attractive and, as I understand, very single. I'm not suggesting you cheat on Felicity. That's for sure!"

Felicity was Levi's live-in love object, and she was known to have a red-hot temper whenever she suspected Levi of cheating. The most serious incident happened when Levi fell under Libby Thomas's spell and became her personal sex slave. Felicity's rage disregarded all boundaries when she plotted to get even with Levi and to hurt Libby in any way she could think of.

Levi said, "Leroy, don't you know that this ole country boy learned his lesson with that whole Libby fiasco? Well, I sure 'nuff did! My sorry ass isn't ever gonna do anything that dumb again! No, never!"

The sheriff smiled as he patted Levi on the back, and they entered the conference room. The sheriff shook his head when he saw Levi gush in the presence of Jeannie Wishart. Levi immediately sat next to her and gave her a once-over.

Wishart slowly turned her head and looked at Levi. "Well, what a surprise! Thought I heard through the grapevine you have been in sexual rehab. Ever since your girlfriend beat your butt for being with another woman."

Levi turned beet red as he digested what she had said. Before he could utter a word, the sheriff called the meeting to order. "Thanks, you all, for being here this morning to share exactly what we have on the double homicide we are working on. I have fielded innumerable calls and e-mails from Carroll County residents; many are terribly frightened by that mess in the alley."

Jim Craig looked around the room and said, "Listen, let me cut to the chase. All my informants are singing the same tune. Estrada and his gang are responsible for the killings. A few of my birds have chirped that Estrada was sick and tired of his soldiers being knocked off by Akers and his henchmen. According to what I was told, the hit was sanctioned by none other than Joaquín Guzmán Loera—that is, El Chapo himself.

"Estrada, or 'Duke,' as he likes his minions to call him, wouldn't have the balls to pull off this level of hit without Guzmán's approval and support. My inside sources told me that while they don't think Akers's organization will retaliate, Guzmán has promised that more soldiers from his organization will jump in if needed."

The sheriff rubbed his forehead before he said, "Well, that's a wonderful possibility in our normally peaceful Carroll County. All hell could now break loose if our local drug-pushing idiots want to up the ante and start killing more people."

Wishart said, "Gentlemen, we are losing the war on drugs. The scourge of drug abuse has battered states across the country. Deaths from overdoses now outstrip those from traffic crashes in Carroll County, as well as in Galax County, Grayson County, and the bordering counties in North Carolina.

"A little history, gentlemen. Let's go back to October 17, 1984, when that Beechcraft Bonanza crashed on Fancy Gap Mountain in the fog. Well, there was five hundred forty pounds of some damn good marijuana on that plane. One Wallace 'Squirrel' Thrasher, from just up the road in Pulaski, owned that plane. Wallace was involved with the Mexican drug lords way back in those days.

"Well, there were two people on that plane that night. The pilot was killed. But one Nelson King somehow survived the crash. He hooked up with Thrasher right after the crash and drove him to a hospital in Florida.

"He was married to Olga Thrasher, who was known as the 'Black Widow.' She got that nickname because she hired a hit man to kill King. Well, she worked out a deal with prosecutors. A deal that kept her out of prison."

Levi put his hand up. "So, what happened to Thrasher?"

Wishart smiled. "After he took King to Florida, he disappeared. There were so many rumors as to where he was hiding. Many thought the Mexicans were hiding him somewhere in Mexico. Olga claimed she had evidence he had died in a plane crash in Belize. That didn't wash with the authorities; they believed he was still alive. As a matter of fact, several retired DEA agents still believe he is alive and probably in Belize.

"As to Olga, she remarried and left the Commonwealth of Virginia. There is no evidence Thrasher ever tried to contact her. As far as the government is concerned, the case is closed. So, let's shift gears and get back to today. We need to understand exactly what audience keeps the drug cartels interested in Southwest Virginia.

"Listen, we are not talking about poor African Americans or Hispanic folks addicted to heroin or prescription drugs.

Our first responders in these counties all carry the hand-held device Evzio, which delivers a single dose of naloxone, a medication that reverses the effects of an overdose. It is often used on those middle- and upper-class folks who have stopped breathing or lost consciousness from opioid overdoses.

"What that translates to, fellas, is this. Estrada and his small army have a burgeoning business here in the hills of Southwest Virginia and in the border counties in North Carolina. The DEA estimates these bad boys send back several millions of dirty dollars through their money-laundering channels to Guzmán and his cronies.

"So, it's as simple as any supply-and-demand business challenge. The demand in our respective jurisdictions continues to go up and up—with no end in sight. No socioeconomic group is immune. The cost of good heroin is so cheap and the supply so plentiful that more people than we could have ever imagined are imprisoned in their addictions.

"Do understand that this is not the first time we have had to deal with these lowlifes. Every time we bring them in for something, they lawyer up with the most expensive talent in Virginia. Those lawyers find a way to always get them out… and out quickly."

The room fell silent for a long minute before Jim Craig said, "Levi, did you understand all the big words from Jeannie?" Craig stopped talking and had a smug expression.

The sheriff was taken aback by Craig's comments. He waited a moment before clearing his throat. Before he could utter a word, Levi held up his hand and said, "Jimmy, I'm sure your sorry ass should have firsthand knowledge of all that, buddy."

"OK, Blackburn, pray tell us what you mean by that."

Levi grinned from ear to ear. "Well, Jimmy, do you mind answering a particular question: When do you expect your wife to get out of rehab, buddy?"

The sheriff jumped from his seat and held up his hands. "All right, you two! Enough of this childish, unprofessional crap! I don't ever want to hear anything like that from either of you! Do you both understand?"

Craig let the anger drain before he replied. "I understand, Sheriff. It won't happen again."

Levi wiped the smirk off his face. "OK, Sheriff, I got it. Won't happen again."

Wishart leaned over, smiled at Levi, and said, "*Good one, Levi*!"

☆ ☆ ☆

Libby Thomas finished working on her last business transaction of the day. Her banking empire now stretched from Virginia to Key West, Florida. *Forbes* had tagged her as one of the ten wealthiest women in the country.

None of that mattered to her, though. As she stood and backed away from her desk, she looked out the massive windows in her office and gazed at the acres and acres of green rolling pastures. Many of her prized horses were grazing on the verdant fields, which stretched for miles and miles.

She had been distracted all afternoon by the recurring memory of seeing Quinn McSpain at the deli. While she kept her sexual desires tamed with exotic dalliances with whoever struck her fancy, her deep attraction to McSpain had come back to roost after seeing him that afternoon.

The thought lingered as she walked over to the rack of wines set on the far wall of her office. She slowly glanced through the hundreds of bottles before settling on one. In the next moment, the 2011 Screaming Eagle Second Flight Cabernet was upright on the wine counter.

She glided the corkscrew gently into the cork; she then placed the bottle between her legs and applied a forceful tug. The cork slid from the bottle's mouth. She examined the small red circle on the bottom of the cork before she set it aside.

Her left hand reached for the decanter on the far end of the table. She knew this cult wine needed some air to let the beauty inside escape. Within a moment, the bottle was empty, and the wine was gently settling into the decanter.

After setting down the empty bottle, she reached for her wineglass of choice. She slowly tipped the decanter and watched the wine fall into her glass. She stopped midstream, sensing a presence at the door of the office. Without looking up, she said, “Artimus, I hope your boots are clean before you come into my space.”

Artimus Bunker, her trainer, realized she had seen his reflection on her wineglass. He slowly walked toward her and said, “Libby, you’re lucky this ole alcoholic doesn’t drink ’cause I sure might enjoy some of that grape juice you’re pouring.”

Libby set the decanter down and looked at him. “Sit yourself down, old man. We need to talk.”

Artimus smiled as he sat in the chair next to her. It was by the big windows.

Libby poured a tall glass of sweet tea, which she passed to him, and then she sat too. He began to say something, but she held up her hand. He stopped for a moment, and she took a slow sip of the wine. She swirled it in her mouth before swallowing. She smiled at him and said, “Artimus, someone in California did all the work, from cradle to grave, to make this wine as great as it is. Few people will be fortunate enough to ever taste a wine as great as this one is.” Libby smiled and set her glass down. “What brings you to see me at this time of day? Are my prized possessions out in the pasture OK? Please tell me you have found the next Belle o’ Fire!”

Artimus took a long, slow sip of his tea. “Libby, you know damn well there will never be another filly like our Belle. We were blessed to have that horse when we did. She gave it her all, and that is all we could have ever asked of her. I know what you’re thinking, woman: you would love to find another filly. Well, that isn't going to happen, and if you think it will, you need to find another trainer."

She digested this as she took another sip of wine. "Damn you, Artimus. You're right. I've been in denial for way too long. Sure, I'd love to have another filly, but I'll be realistic and believe we should find the best horse that money can buy. But don't even think of leaving me! You are the only man I can count on, for Christ's sake! Together we can get this job done."

Libby reached for the decanter and refilled her glass. As she took another sip, tears rolled down her cheeks. Artimus stood, leaned down, and gave her a hug. She continued to sob before she suddenly stood. "All right," she said, "get the hell out of here and start looking for our next star! And listen, old man, I only wish you were a younger stud yourself. You could have helped me in other places as well!"

With that, Artimus stood and started to back away. "Libby, if you would have known me as a young man, you would have worked for me!"

She watched him leave her office. She took the wine bottle and filled her glass. She walked to the massive windows that faced her pastures. The peace and serenity of seeing her horses in the pastures washed over her. She knew something in her life was missing, though. She lacked the inner peace she had thought money could buy, but no matter what she bought, the emptiness never went away.

In a moment, she spun around and sat behind her desk. She brought her computer back to life, gazed at the screen saver, lifted her wineglass to her lips, and blew a kiss to the image. It was a picture of *Quinn McSpain.*

CHAPTER 13

Tommie Cruz sat behind his desk and rubbed his eyes. He had been working for hours on new apps for an important client in Seattle. His clients loved the work Alphonse Pickering produced for them. Tommie smiled as he signed off as Pickering and powered his system down.

Though it was only four in the afternoon, he had decided what he had to do next. He stood and looked around his inner sanctum. His gaze stopped at a small and clear glass bottle, which was placed at eye level on a shelf. He slowly and carefully picked it up and looked closely at the small object in it.

His gaze turned wicked. He set the bottle back down. Without hesitation, he stormed out of his inner sanctum. As he passed through the threshold, he shouted, "Close!" The doors immediately swung shut, and an interior locking system bolted into place.

Without hesitation, he opened his bedside drawer and gripped his Smith & Wesson Bodyguard. No need for the Taurus. He had planned to take them both out at close range. He checked the clip as he flew down the stairs to his garage.

Once inside, he placed his pistol in the right saddlebag on his motorcycle. The garage door slid down as he negotiated the alley behind his house in Galax. He was soon heading to Highway 58.

The warm afternoon felt good on his bare arms and shoulders, and his sleeveless tank top rippled in the breeze. He loved driving up and down the long hills on Highway 58. He slowed as the light at the intersection of Highway 52 turned red. A car, planning to turn left onto Highway 52, pulled up alongside him.

Four teenage girls looked at him, and the girl closest to him rolled down her window and whistled. When he didn't acknowledge her, she pulled up her tank top, exposing her ample cream-colored breasts.

As the light turned green, Tommie accelerated through the turn and onto Highway 52. He didn't offer the slightest look at the topless girl in the car. He was only focused on what he planned to do with Quinn McSpain and Louisa Hawke.

The girl grinned, flipped him the bird, and yelled, "*Fuck you, asshole*!"

☆ ☆ ☆

Louisa finished gathering some wood for the fireplace and walked upstairs from the lower level. She could hear voices from the living room and realized the television was on. At the top of the landing, she saw Quinn watching a recap of the latest political news.

The commentators were describing the latest polls, which indicated that Donald Trump was now in a virtual tie with Hillary Clinton in the national polls. Louisa sat on the edge of the couch and looked at Quinn. “Is your guy Donald still making an ass of himself?”

Quinn took a moment to smile, fully understanding they both had seats at opposite ends of the political table. Louisa was a staunch Democrat, and Quinn was a moderate Republican. She wasn’t totally enamored with Hillary Clinton, but she had let go of any hope for Bernie Sanders since he had been hacked by the Democratic National Committee.

“Well, my dearest Hillary lover,” said Quinn, “you know darn well that Trump is simply the unexplainable aberration of this political season. He’s just as crazy as Bernie Sanders, who gave your gal Hillary, the e-mail maven, very unexpected fits during his effort to kick her to the curb—until the DNC screwed him. I just can’t comprehend why your former employer never brought criminal charges against her.”

Louisa smirked. “Listen, my former compadres at the bureau have worked hard and long to see if any of that e-mail business on her private server warranted any criminal charges. They sure as hell wouldn’t have shirked their responsibilities just because she is running for president!”

Quinn never turned his head. “You don’t really believe that, do you? You know the lackeys who run the bureau jump whenever Obama or Hillary says jump. It's a pure shame that J. Edgar Hoover isn't still in charge of that operation. He must be rolling over in his grave!"

Louisa stood and folded her arms. "McSpain, for a bright person, you sometimes say the dumbest things. You know damn well the FBI has never been the political pawn of any president. That was different in your corporate life, where the likes of Donald Trump and his cronies simply stole millions from those who did business with them."

Quinn stood and looked at her. "My dearest, I must flee your political fantasies and get going to the Dollar General. I'm cooking tonight, and I need some spices for the meal and little ole you!"

She looked away as he headed to the door. "Don't forget the toilet paper for all the crap coming out of—"

Quinn let the screen door shut behind him and never heard *her last comment.*

☆ ☆ ☆

Estrada and Medina didn't say a word as they drove down Highway 52. They were heading back into Hillsville. Estrada realized they needed to do whatever they could to identify the Mennonite woman and the little girl who had witnessed them killing Akers and his compatriot.

Their mole who worked in the sheriff's department could not provide any kind of useful information pertaining to the progress of the investigation. Estrada had even upped the amount of money he was willing to pay for any useful information. Nothing came from any of their sources.

Medina said, "Duke, I hope we get lucky tonight and find the woman we are looking for. I know the local cops will be working with the fucking DEA and the state police."

Estrada continued to drive. He slowed as they got to the south side of Hillsville. "Roger, just relax. They ain't got jack shit on us. If they did, we would have had visitors. The woman and the little girl have not talked to the police...not yet."

He slowed as he entered the back alley behind the Deutsche Pantry. They both knew it had been closed for at least fifteen minutes. They parked within twenty feet of the old Ford pickup. Within two minutes, the back door of the restaurant opened, and a woman stepped outside.

She walked down the steps leading off the porch and headed to the pickup. In a matter of seconds, Estrada and Medina leaped from their truck and ambushed the woman. Medina had a piece of duct tape waiting, and he used it to cover her mouth.

She fought back as both men tried to restrain her. She dropped the keys to her truck as they struggled. Medina pulled a syringe from his pocket and stuck it in her left thigh; the drug quickly worked its way through her system and diminished her effort to resist.

Estrada and Medina pulled her into the back seat of their truck. Her breathing became shallow as the drug saturated her system and completely relaxed her muscles.

Estrada slowly drove his truck through the backstreets of Hillsville. He was looking side to side to see if anyone had witnessed the abduction. No one had. Medina rocked back and forth in the passenger seat, anticipating what was to come. Estrada drove out of town and *smiled.*

* * *

Quinn smiled as he drove his Ram out of the driveway. He headed to the Blue Ridge Parkway. He knew Louisa supported Hillary Clinton, and she was adamant in her belief Clinton would be a good president.

They had enjoyed some spirited debates when the candidates were competing for delegates in the primary states. While he had supported Marco Rubio, it was becoming apparent that Donald Trump had tapped into a national vein of disgust and unhappiness in the electorate. That, he thought, was a disturbing turn of events.

He turned the Ram through the uphill curve on the parkway at mile marker 196, and he thought he saw a buck on the left side of the road. What he didn't see going in the opposite direction on State Road 608 was a single motorcycle slowing to make a turn. The man on the motorcycle had failed to see Quinn too.

* * *

Medina punched in the usual code. They were within one hundred yards of the bridge over Big Reed Island Creek.

The gate opened just as the front wheels of the truck hit the beginning of the bridge.

Peggy Neufeld began to stir in the back seat of the truck as they crossed the bridge. She saw little light through the blanket that covered her. She tried to move her hands but soon realized they were taped together. Her feet were not bound in any way.

She felt the motion of the truck abruptly stop. Two men were talking in Spanish in the front seat. The talking stopped as the truck's front doors opened. The door closest to her feet opened, and a man took hold of her legs and pulled her forward.

Once they were outside the truck, Medina pushed her in the direction another man was taking. She was still weak from the drug in her system and could not focus well. Her legs wobbled as Medina pushed her along.

Estrada stopped at the doors of a distant barn. He unlocked the doors and slid them open. As soon as Medina and the woman passed through, he closed the doors and locked them from the inside.

Through her drowsy eyes, Neufeld saw what she thought was a hay barn. The faces of her two captives were still a bit blurry. The larger of the two men opened an inner door in the barn, and Medina pushed her into the inner room.

Estrada flicked on the lights. She could see a solitary table and no more than four chairs. Several pairs of shackles were on the table. She also saw many whips hanging from hooks on a far wall.

Medina sat her in one of the chairs. She tried to concentrate on his face as he cut the tape around her wrists. He then ripped the tape from her mouth. She felt the circulation return to her hands and arms.

The second man came to the table and sat opposite to her. He placed several water bottles on the table. Estrada looked at her. "Drink some water," he said.

She slowly reached across the table and took a bottle. Peggy Neufeld's mind raced as she looked at both men. Within a moment, she realized she had seen them both in the Deutsche Pantry. She felt faint. The realization set in that these men were involved in the murders at the Pantry. Tears began to run down her cheeks as she drank from the water bottle in front of her.

Estrada smiled as he inched his chair closer to the table. "What is your name?" he asked.

"It's Peggy. My name is Peggy Neufeld. Why have you brought me here?"

Estrada stood. "Well, Peggy, you are a very smart person, but I will keep this as simple as I can. I need to know the name of the woman who was working at the Pantry when those men were killed. All I need is her name. Nothing else."

Neufeld knew Hope Showalter and her daughter had witnessed the horrific murders. She had also figured out these men were probably the ones who were responsible for killing the other men.

"Do you have a family, Peggy?" Medina asked.

She shook her head. "No, I live with my parents."

Estrada looked at her. "Do you have a cell phone?"

She looked down. "No, my parents haven't allowed me to have one."

Both men watched her as she continued to digest their request. She knew that if she gave them Hope's name, they would surely kill Hope and Hannah. She also knew these men would do whatever they needed to do to get the names they wanted. Her hand trembled as she drank more water.

"Do you have a bathroom I could use?" she asked.

Estrada nodded to Medina, who stood, took her by the arm, and led her out of the room. Once in the main part of the barn, he took her to the far side and opened the door to the toilet. He flicked on the light and led her in. He smiled as he closed the door behind him.

She sat on the toilet and thought of what she could do to survive. The fact she had seen them and could identify them was not lost on her. She must try *to escape.*

☆ ☆ ☆

Louisa turned off the television and put the remote on the counter. She realized politics was an area in which she and Quinn were polar opposites. While he usually maintained some flexibility in most day-to-day issues, Louisa knew Quinn was not happy with the course the country had been on for the last eight years.

While she supported Hillary Clinton as the most experienced candidate, she still harbored certain trust issues. This had dogged Clinton throughout her campaign. She knew Quinn didn't need to know how she felt about all that, though.

She looked out the kitchen window and saw the sun beginning to set in the western sky. All the day's projects and work in her garden had taken their toll. Within a moment, she opened the wine cooler and took out a new bottle of Angel Chardonnay.

Wineglass in hand, she went to the bedroom and slipped out of her clothes and into a terry cloth robe. She was certain the hot tub was fired up and ready to be enjoyed. She went outside on the lower deck, set down her wineglass, and took off the top of the tub.

Wisps of steam rolled up from the water as she threw off her robe and climbed into the tub. She wallowed in the immediate sense of relief as the hot water and the throbbing jets massaged her body.

She sat up for a moment to take another sip of her wine and to take in the sun, which was getting closer to the western ridge. This was her favorite time of day, and she only wished Quinn was there to enjoy it with her. The very thought of him stirred a *lustful moan*.

✡ ✡ ✡

Peggy Neufeld acted instinctively when Medina led her from the bathroom. A piece of firewood was leaning against the door. In one fell swoop, she reached down, snatched the piece of wood, and swung it at Medina.

Her aim was true, and she hit Medina on the back of his head. He staggered for a moment before falling to the barn floor with a thud. Without a moment's hesitation, she bolted toward the barn doors.

Estrada was checking e-mails on his iPhone when he thought he heard something fall in the barn. He bolted to the door, only to see Medina stretched out in front of him. Blood was trickling from the back of his skull. He moaned as he rolled over and opened his eyes. "That bitch hit me good."

Estrada looked at the bloodied piece of wood lying on the floor next to Medina. "Get up, Roger! We need to catch that bitch and teach her a lesson."

When Neufeld was outside the barn, she squinted through the darkness and saw the lights on in the houses ahead of her. She instinctively knew she must run in the other direction. Through experience, she knew the North Star lighted the way to true north. She quickly found the North Star in the northern sky and ran as fast as she could in that direction.

Estrada stopped at the barn's entrance, opened a wall box, and took out the hardwired phone. The phone in the main house rang only once, and Tony Esquivel answered it.

Estrada screamed, "Get Luis and come to the barn right now! The churchwoman has escaped!"

Within a moment, Esquivel and Solis tore out of the house and headed to the barn. They soon caught up to Medina, who was behind Estrada. Blood was dripping from the laceration on the back of his head. They both passed him and caught up with Estrada.

Esquivel, who was already breathing hard, asked, "Boss, how far ahead is she?"

Estrada picked up the pace. "She ain't too far. We will catch the bitch."

Peggy Neufeld had to stop to catch her breath. The path was steep and was getting steeper. She was losing sight of the stars through the thickening clouds. The sounds of voices getting closer and closer startled her. Fear took over, and she bolted to higher ground. Within a few steps, her right foot caught a tree root, and she went down hard, feeling her right ankle twist. Taking a deep breath, she pulled herself up by holding on to a young sapling. As soon as she put her weight on her leg, she knew it had been severely strained or broken.

Just as she reached out to grab another tree, she felt the power of a strong grip on her arm. Her struggle to free herself was futile. Others had arrived, and several arms were holding her down.

The cloud cover cleared, allowing her to see the man standing over her. Estrada smiled and kicked her in the stomach. She tried to cover her head as he repeatedly kicked her from head to toe.

She writhed in pain as the beating continued. He suddenly stopped kicking her. Estrada slowly dropped to one knee and bent close to her left ear. "No, I'm not going to kill you here. I'm going to take you back to the barn, and the boys will have their way with you. You will have plenty of time and good reasons to tell me who the woman and the child are."

By this time, Medina had joined the party. His face was covered with blood. He seethed as he looked at her, and Estrada understood his anger. "Not now, Roger! You will get your chance to do as you wish with this bitch."

Solis and Esquivel each grabbed one of her arms and began to drag her down the mountain. Peggy bumped along. She masked her pain with the only thought that dogged her. *I am going to die.*

CHAPTER 14

Tara Neufeld paced in her kitchen, constantly looking at the clock above her refrigerator. She finally walked into the living room and looked at her husband, who was reading. "Samson, I'm really worried about Peggy. She should have been home two hours ago."

Samson Neufeld looked up from his book. "Have you called Hope to see if she closed the Pantry on time?"

Sara frowned. "I did, and Hope has no reason to think Peggy didn't. I called the Pantry, and there was no answer."

Samson suddenly bemoaned the fact his daughter did not have a cell phone. He closed his book and stood. "Let's go to the Pantry and see what there is to see."

Samson looked straight ahead as he drove. He thought of the possibilities that lay ahead in Hillsville. None of them were good.

Within five minutes, they turned onto Court Street and turned left into the alley beside the Pantry. The headlights settled on Peggy's old Ford F-150 pickup. They both got out and walked over to the truck. Samson tried to open the driver's side door. It was locked.

Tara walked up to the back door of the Pantry and turned the doorknob. It was locked.

Samson went to his truck and took his flashlight from the center console. He turned it on and began to search the ground around the truck. He shone the beam on the pickup's bed, but nothing caught his eye.

He walked over to the driver's side and looked on the ground by the running board. A shiny object caught his eye under the running board. He bent down on one knee and reached under the truck.

By then, Tara was standing next to him. "Have you found anything?"

Samson stood and held Peggy's keys in the palm of his hand. He trembled as he said, "There is something terribly wrong here, Tara. Our daughter has been taken."

She placed her hands in his, and tears streamed down her cheeks. "What should we do, Samson? I don't understand this."

He embraced her and whispered, "We must go the sheriff's office right now. They need to be involved as soon as possible. Something terrible has happened here, and we must pray for *our daughter's life.*"

☆ ☆ ☆

When Tommie Cruz was satisfied that his motorcycle was hidden from view, he tucked his pistol into his belt holster and zipped up his Windbreaker. He knew exactly where he was going through the thick woods. He chose a longer route to get to McSpain's home; he did not want to come close to other cabins in the area.

The sun was lowering over the ridgeline and western slopes and was casting shadows, through which Tommie walked slowly. Within ten minutes, he was within one hundred yards of the south side of the house. He crouched in tall brush, where he could see the lower level around the hot tub. He also noticed McSpain's truck was not in the driveway.

Louisa languished in the swirling water and reached for her wineglass. She giggled when she picked up her empty glass. Without hesitation, she stood and stretched her arms and legs. Golden water droplets cascaded off her body as she reached for the wine bottle.

Cruz watched from the clump of short pines he was hiding in. He noticed her tanned and lithe body as she poured wine into her glass. He reached down and slowly pulled the Bodyguard pistol from his pocket.

Louisa sat on the edge of the tub, taking in the final glow of the evening sunset. She smiled, slipped her leg over the edge of the tub, and sank back into the steaming and bubbling water. Engulfed in warmth, she thought of Quinn and what she would do to him when he returned.

Tommie Cruz paused for a moment and slipped his pistol back into his pocket. He reached back and unsheathed his Flamesteed hunting knife. He felt his rage and hatred for both McSpain and Hawke start to bubble and boil. The thought of slitting Louisa's throat simmered as he crawled from his cover, up the grassy slope, and to the hot tub.

He held his emotions in check as he inched closer to his quarry. He now could see the top of Louisa's head and her long red hair as she soaked in the tub. Her eyes were closed.

Seconds slowly ticked by. He was within two feet of the tub. He raised himself to a crouch. The time to pounce was at hand. At that very moment, he caught the sound of a vehicle coming up the gravel road. It was coming toward the cabin.

He was not the only one who heard the noise on the road. Louisa propped herself up in the tub and saw Quinn pull into the driveway. She held up her half-empty wineglass and waved. Quinn blew the horn in recognition.

Tommie Cruz had to make a quick decision. He started to put his knife back into the sheath with one hand as he reached for his pistol with the other. He stopped himself, feeling consumed with desire to stab her.

Louisa was startled; she saw Cruz's reflection in her wine-glass. With catlike reflexes, she reached over the other side of the tub and grabbed the half-empty wine bottle. In one fell swoop, she yelled and swung the bottle toward the body lunging in her direction.

Louisa's swing was true. She hit Cruz squarely on top of his head. He fell back toward the steep embankment at the back of the lower deck. He dropped his knife while trying to slow his free fall down the side of the hill.

Quinn pivoted when he heard Louisa scream. He saw her climbing out of the hot tub with a wine bottle in one hand. He also saw a body rolling down the side of the hill. Instinctively he reached into the center console of his truck and grabbed his revolver. Within ten bounds, he was beside the hot tub and Louisa. "Are you OK?" he asked.

They both watched the body stop rolling at the bottom of the hill.

"I'm OK. Now get down there and deal with that motherfucker. I'll call the sheriff and get some clothes on."

Quinn braced himself. He firmly planted each of his steps on the downhill slope, and he focused on the person who was now crouching and looking in his direction.

Tommie felt a throb in the back of his head. He saw McSpain heading in his direction. His right hand raised the Bodyguard, and he quickly squeezed off two rounds in Quinn's direction. He then calculated that he needed a moment or two to reach the tree line in front of him.

Quinn dived when he saw the pistol pointed in his direction. That proved fortunate. The two bullets whizzed by him. Each was less than a foot from his head. After he regained his balance and looked up, he saw the person running toward the tree line.

He held his pistol in his right hand, set the butt in his left palm, and squeezed off three rounds. He knew the two-and-a-half-inch 410 load was the first to go. Two .45 ACPs followed. He watched the tree line as he ran in a half-crouched position.

Cruz felt the impact of the shots fired in his direction. Running through the woods, he realized McSpain had considerably more firepower than he did. His path, which traced a wide circle, was now taking him far away from where he had parked his motorcycle.

Quinn entered the tree line and stopped to listen for any movement in the forest. He stood and listened, noticing the day had become dark. There was nothing to hear. He turned and saw all the lights of the cabin being turned on. He heard a siren getting closer from the state road.

Within minutes, he was climbing the last steep incline to the driveway. He was greeted by several cars of the sheriff's deputies, which were approaching. An unmarked cruiser was the first to arrive.

Louisa ran out the back door to the driveway to meet Quinn. She jumped into his arms and hugged him with all her might. They looked at each other and were lost in time until Sheriff Jefferson stepped up to them.

"Jeez, you two. Tell me what the hell happened here," he said.

Louisa looked at Quinn and the sheriff. "It was all crazy. I was sitting in the hot tub and sipping my wine, and then I saw the reflection of a man no more than two feet from me. I grabbed my wine bottle and swung it in his direction. He must have sprung at me at that very moment 'cause I scored a direct hit on his noggin. That was just when Quinn got back and went after him."

Quinn said, "He rolled down the hill and then got off a couple of shots at me with his pistol. Judging by the sound of it, I'm willing to bet it was a small caliber. Something in the three eighty range. Then he fled to the tree line and into the woods."

Sheriff Jefferson looked at Louisa. "Did you see the gun in his hand while he was by the tub?"

Louisa shook her head. "He had a knife in his hand when he sprang at me. That I'm sure of."

Quinn looked off into the distance before he said, "Where is the wine bottle now?"

Louisa took his hand and headed down the path to the hot tub. The sheriff followed. She stopped in front of the side table, which was on the near side of the hot tub.

Leroy took his flashlight and examined all sides of the bottle. "Well, whoever this madman is, he left a fair amount of blood on this bottle."

Louisa looked at them both. "So, who wants in on my bet that this blood will match that asshole who shot at you on the parkway?"

Both Leroy and Quinn nodded their agreement. Quinn took the sheriff's flashlight and moved to the grass line nearest the hot tub. He swung the flashlight side to side and took small steps down the hill.

Louisa and the sheriff watched as Quinn halted and stooped. “Leroy,” he said, “get an evidence bag and bring it to me.”

The sheriff ran up to his cruiser and quickly returned. He rejoined Quinn and Louisa on the side of the hill.

Leroy slipped his gloves on as he neared Quinn. Once there, he squatted to get a better look at what Quinn had found. “Wow, that is one glitzy knife,” the sheriff said.

“I don’t think I’ve ever seen one like that,” said Louisa.

Quinn looked at them both. “It looks like a Flamesteed hunting knife. I saw one many years ago, and this one looks a lot like the one I saw. They are very collectible and expensive. And I don’t think there are many around.”

Leroy thought about what Quinn had said. “So, what we have is a knife that should be traceable. This not-your-run-of-the-mill hunting knife was not bought at Walmart. So, I bet we can talk to whoever made this masterpiece.” The sheriff slipped the knife into the evidence bag and looked at them both. “Listen, you two, this is getting crazy. This fool is hell-bent on killing you. I just don’t think he is going away. He wants both of you dead and won’t stop till you *are*!”

* * *

Peggy Neufeld slipped in and out of consciousness. She slowly opened her eyes and saw four men looking at her. Her arms and legs were stretched to their limits; she was bound spread-eagle on a mat in the barn. She shivered. A chill came over her naked body. Fear came next when the men began to undress.

Estrada knelt and gently brushed the hair from her face. "Now is the time to tell us who the woman and the child are. If you don't, others like you will suffer. I will find your mother and father and hurt them as well. This is your decision, Peggy."

Tears came to her eyes in the seconds before she spit in his face. He slowly got up from his knees and stood. He waved at Medina. "You're first."

Peggy closed her eyes and prayed as hard *as she ever had.*

☆ ☆ ☆

Tommie Cruz sat in tall bushes for at least three hours before deciding it was safe to leave and drive back to his house in Galax. The blood on his head had dried, but the throbbing headache was intense. He now focused on taking every back road he could for the twenty or so miles he had to travel.

Darkness was his friend as he wove his way through deserted streets. He soon found himself slowly driving into the back alley behind his house and parking his motorcycle in his garage. He looked both ways down the street before closing and locking the doors.

As he climbed the stairs to his kitchen, he berated himself for failing to kill his prey. He simmered as he looked at his head in the bathroom mirror and saw the gash on the back of his head. His greatest concern was that he had lost his knife by the hot tub. He understood that the police would probably trace the knife to the artist who had made it. That didn't bother him because that person had never heard of Tommie Cruz. However, he knew the knife could be a problem.

His attention soon shifted to the bank of small screens monitoring all points of entry to his house. Missy's smiling face was framed by the camera that covered the side door to his house. For a moment, he didn't know if he wanted to see Missy.

As soon as he scanned the camera up and down Missy's torso, he knew he would let her in. The tan trench coat she was wearing sealed the deal. He pushed an access button that unlocked the door. He watched her strut down the hall in her black high heels.

He turned down the room lights when Missy entered the room. She smiled as she walked across the room and into his arms. "Oh shit, Tommie. Your head is all bloodied up! What the hell happened to you, baby?"

Tommie looked down at Missy's wide-open trench coat. Her natural assets were on display. "Listen, baby, I had a little accident. That's all."

Missy shook her head. "Listen, fella, that is a big gash. I can clean it up and put some bandages on it, but you might need some stitches."

He wrapped his arms around her waist and gave her a hard squeeze. "You just do the best you can, and I'll see how I feel tomorrow."

She pushed him away, smirked, and said, "Listen, you dumb shit, you could have a concussion and not know it right know. And that shit could get worse."

Tommie smiled as she washed the back of his head with alcohol. She fashioned a circular patch and carefully set it in place with tape. She was satisfied that the bleeding had stopped. He watched her go to the freezer and take out an ice pack; she wrapped it in a thin dish towel she found in a drawer.

With her free hand, she took one of his and led him to his bedroom. She then had him sit on his bed. She reached over, fluffed several of his pillows, and pushed him back on the bed, where she made him sit straight. "Now, Tommie," she said, "I want you to hold that ice pack on your head for at least fifteen minutes."

He complied and kept the bag on his head. He used both hands. He smiled as she backed away from the bed with a sultry smile on her face.

The trench coat slowly slipped from her as she made slow, rhythmic movements with her hips and shoulders. Her hands fondled her creamy, tanned breasts; she massaged both nipples between her fingertips.

Tommie watched and soon forgot about the throbbing knot on his head. He felt his blood diverting to his lower extremity, which was quickly coming to life. Missy crawled on the bottom of the bed and slowly pulled Tommie's jeans off. She ran her hands slowly up his legs but stopped within inches of his manhood. Tommie started to move his hands down from the ice pack on his head.

"Stop that right now," growled Missy, "and get your hands back on that ice pack."

He smiled and complied, resting both hands on top of his head. "Oh, baby," he said, "you can keep that up all night 'cause I'm feeling better and better!"

Missy sat on his chest and moved his hands off his scalp. She turned the ice pack over and set it in place. Tommie moaned. Her scent overwhelmed him, and he licked his dry lips. He knew what *he needed to do next.*

✲ ✲ ✲

As soon as Leroy Jefferson hung up the phone, it rang again. He was working late and feeling eager to go home. The receptionist at the entrance to the sheriff's department was calling. "Sheriff, a Samson and Tara Neufeld are here to see you."

Leroy glanced over at his appointment book to see if he had forgotten an appointment. He hadn't. He did recall he had met the Neufelds at a large gathering the Mennonite community had held for him during his reelection campaign. He knew the two were well respected by their peers, as well as throughout Carroll County.

He didn't hesitate when he instructed the receptionist to send the Neufelds to his office. He glanced at his calendar and realized he was free for the next hour or so. Just at that moment, he heard a knock at his door. Leroy stood and walked around his desk to open the door. He greeted Samson and his wife as they stepped into his office.

"Sheriff," said Samson, "we sure hate to bother you, but I'm afraid we need your help."

"No bother at all, folks. Please sit down and make yourselves comfortable. It's been a while since I've see you, but by the looks on your faces, my gut is telling me this is not a social call." He closed his office door and sat behind his desk.

"Sheriff," continued Samson, "Peggy, our daughter, works at the Deutsche Pantry, and she didn't come home when she should have. We waited a little bit, but when we realized the Pantry was closed and she hadn't come home yet, we drove over to see if she was still there. Well, when we got there, her old truck was there, but she was nowhere to be found. I found her keys on the ground by the driver's door. Sheriff, I think something is terribly wrong here. We are both worried sick."

Leroy instinctively agreed. Something was terribly wrong with this picture. "I have to ask. Did you call her?"

Tara said, "We tried calling the Pantry, but no one answered the phone. And she doesn't have a cell phone, Sheriff."

Leroy stood and walked to the office windows. He thought Levi Blackburn might still be at the station. He was probably at his desk. He knew his senior investigator should be in the room to hear this story. Seemingly on cue, he saw Levi stand at his desk and grab his hat. He was preparing to leave.

The sheriff cracked his door open. "Not so fast, Levi. I need you in my office."

Levi pretended not to hear him; he took two steps to leave.

"Levi, not so quick! Need you in here. Now!"

Levi stopped in his tracks and pivoted in the direction of the sheriff's office. He smiled as he looked at Leroy. "Why, sir, I will be right in!"

When Levi entered the office, the sheriff introduced him to the Neufelds. "Folks, Levi is our senior investigator at the sheriff's department. Tell him what you just told me."

Levi listened as Samson Neufeld recounted all they knew from the past twenty-four hours. He scribbled some notes on his notepad as they spoke. When Samson finished, Levi looked at Leroy and said, "Sheriff, I think we need to get someone over to the Pantry to secure the area around their daughter's pickup truck."

Leroy nodded in agreement, and he stood and left the room.

Levi looked at the Neufelds. "Folks, I need as much information about Peggy as you can give me. First, does she have a cell phone?"

Samson shook his head. "No, Levi. We didn't think she was old enough to have a cell phone. We planned to give her one when she turned eighteen next year."

"OK. So, is there someone who might have met her after work at the Pantry?" asked Levi.

Tara shook her head. "No, Detective. She would have told us if she had made plans to go somewhere after work. She would have called from the Pantry."

"Does she have a boyfriend?" asked Levi.

They both shook their heads. After a moment, Samson sat up in his chair and said, "Peggy certainly has boys and girls she is friendly with at school. She does not have a boyfriend, though."

The door to the office opened, and the sheriff came in and sat at his desk.

Levi jotted down a few more notes. "Now, folks, think back a few days to when those two fellas were killed behind the Pantry. Did Peggy work that day?"

Tara looked at her husband. "Yes, she did work on that dreadful day. She only worked a half day. She came home after lunch."

Samson looked at his wife. "Didn't Hope close on that terrible day?"

Tara nodded in the affirmative.

The sheriff and Levi exchanged a glance. "Are you both sure?" asked the sheriff. "Did Hope Showalter close the restaurant that night?"

Samson said, "We are sure, Sheriff."

Levi spent the next ten minutes getting as much information about Peggy as he could. As Samson and Tara stood to leave, Levi looked at the Neufelds and said, "We will do all we can to find Peggy, but it's important you have all the members in your church ask each other if they might have seen her."

Tara began to sob as she and her husband walked out of the sheriff's office. The sheriff put his hand on her shoulder and said, "We will use every resource to find Peggy."

Samson stopped and looked at the sheriff. "May God be at your side through all of this."

Levi and the sheriff watched them leave and then returned to the office. Levi said, "Did I miss something in here with that whole Hope Showalter thing?"

The sheriff looked out the window as he said, "Levi, I was in the Pantry for lunch a few days after the killings. I spoke to Hope about that terrible mess. I sensed she knew something crucial. That she was holding something back from me. I just had a gut feeling."

"Well, when I interviewed Hope, she told me she locked the place up at closing and hightailed it home to her house in Volunteer Gap. So, you think there might be more to her story than she is letting on?"

"Yes, Levi, and our job is to find out exactly what before more shit *hits the fan*!"

CHAPTER 15

Quinn could sense the tension in Louisa in the days following the attack in their hot tub. He knew all the local police agencies were alerted to the fact that a man might be seeking medical attention for a severe laceration on his head. The hospitals in Galax and Mount Airy had been alerted, as well as those in Winston-Salem and Roanoke. Unfortunately, nothing had been reported so far.

He was mulling everything over when Louisa came back into the kitchen. She had been working in her garden for several hours. Quinn smiled as she washed her hands in the sink. "So, any bounty from your garden for us to share tonight?" he asked.

She turned as she dried off her hands. "Didn't you suggest you were going to treat me to a very special dinner at that new vineyard on Pilot Mountain?"

Quinn stood, walked to the sink, and took her hands. "After everything you have been through lately, we should fly to Paris for dinner. But since I believe you are as hungry as I am, let's head down to Pilot Mountain and have dinner at JOLO, the new place that has some great online reviews."

"Say no more, my love, 'cause I can be out of these jeans, showered, and gussied up in fifteen minutes, providing you don't have a little appetizer in mind before we leave."

Quinn pushed her in the direction of the bedroom. "If I wasn't so darn hungry, I might take you up on that, but the growl I hear in my stomach demands we postpone our carnal desires. We must wait heroically."

Louisa giggled as she dropped her jeans to the floor and took three steps into the shower.

When they were in Quinn's truck and on their way, Louisa watched Quinn negotiate the mountain's curves as he drove south on Highway 52. At times, he reminded her of a teenage as he negotiated those tricky downhill curves without ever touching the brakes.

He was lost in the moment, and they soon reached the bottom of the mountain in Cana. No words were needed. She felt joy, and love fill her heart for this man.

Within twenty minutes, Quinn pulled his truck into JOLO's parking lot. Louisa stepped out and watched Quinn as he came around the corner of the truck. "Wow," she said, "this is a beautiful setting. Look at the great view of Pilot Mountain back there. What a lovely setting. This is impressive."

Quinn saw the front door open, and a man stepped out onto the stoop. The man smiled and waved to them. "Hey," he said, "you two look as if you appreciate the view, but you need to step inside to enjoy the best part…our wine!"

Louisa and Quinn held hands as they walked down the hill and met the man by the door.

"Folks, I'm J. W., and welcome to JOLO winery!"

Quinn and Louisa stopped in front of the beautiful fireplace in the lobby and looked around the tasting room. Louisa smiled as J. W. turned toward them. "This is very nice," she said.

J. W. shook their hands as they introduced themselves. "Folks, this place has been a labor of love. My wife and I moved our family here, hoping and desiring to produce some of the best wines this area would ever see."

Louisa whispered to Quinn, "Did he say his name was J. W. or J. R.? 'Cause he is a hunk!"

Quinn replied, "No, that is not J. R. Ewing."

As they talked, J. W. uncorked a bottle of red wine and poured some in both of their glasses. "This our award-winning Jolotage, which, I'm happy to say, has received rave reviews."

Quinn swirled the wine in his glass and took a small sip. Louisa did the same. She took a moment before she looked at Quinn. "This is very nice," she said, and Quinn nodded in agreement.

J. W. blushed, smiled, and refilled their glasses. For the next few minutes, the three discussed the merits of the wine and how it got from the grapes to their glasses.

Quinn almost forgot how hungry he was until a young lady appeared from the dining room. "Folks, your table is ready," she said.

Quinn stood and offered to shake hands with J. W. "I must say, you have produced a wonderful wine in your Jolotage. My congratulations to you and your team."

J. W. led them into the dining room. At their table, he pulled Louisa's chair back for her. After she and Quinn were seated, J. W. said, "Enjoy your meal, and I certainly hope to see you both again soon."

With that, he smiled and returned to the tasting room.

Louisa smiled, reached over, and took Quinn's hand. She exhaled as she squeezed his hand. "This is exactly what I needed. So, no more politics. I promise. The last week or so has been crazy. Drug lords beheaded in Hillsville and some idiot trying to kill us. What the hell is going on, Quinn?"

Before he could answer, his cell phone rang. He looked at the screen and saw Leroy's name on it. He showed it to Louisa, and she nodded in the affirmative, giving him permission to answer it. "Hello, Leroy. Can you guess where we are?"

The sheriff paused. "Well, I see you are in North Carolina. Probably drinking wine with Louisa somewhere. Listen, I won't be long. I just met with Tara and Samson Neufeld. They informed me their daughter, Peggy, is missing. Well, I'll make a long story short. We found the daughter's truck in the back of the Pantry, and the keys were lying on the ground. She works there and usually comes home after work. You know what I'm thinking, Quinn?"

"I do, Leroy, and it is troublesome. There must be a connection with the killings that happened in the alley. This is not good. Not good at all. Listen, Louisa and I are in Pilot Mountain having dinner. We will call you tomorrow."

"Thanks, Quinn," the sheriff said before hanging up.

Quinn took a long sip of his wine and described to Louisa what Leroy had said. "You know as well as I do," said Quinn, "that the local drug kingpins probably decided it was time for one group to establish dominance. Well, they not only accomplished that but also made a heinous statement."

Louisa took a long sip of wine. "I see where you are going with this. What Leroy just told us would seem to indicate a connection between the killings and the fact Peggy Neufeld is now missing. A person who works at the Pantry has come up missing shortly after two people were killed there."

Quinn nodded in agreement. "For the sake of conversation, it would appear the two events are connected. I'm going to guess someone who works at the Pantry witnessed the murders."

"Exactly, McSpain, and I'm going to bet the killers know that but don't know the identities of the witnesses. Having said all that, I don't see a connection between those killings and whoever is trying to kill us."

They both took long sips of wine before Quinn spoke. "I agree with that. I do think the person trying to kill us has a severe hard-on just for us. But what is the connection that links him to us?"

Louisa looked at the ceiling for a moment. "I'm trying to narrow down the possibilities. It sure as hell could be someone connected to our friendly terrorist, who was somehow connected to our young and deadly scientist. Or it could be someone who still holds a grudge about the killing of Father Tony."

Before Quinn could answer, J. W. approached their table. He was carrying their main course. After he set down the plates, he reached over to the next table, where he had already uncorked a new bottle of wine. "Looks as if you two need some more fruit of the vine to go with dinner."

Quinn and Louisa smiled, but they were both deep in thought. They were ruminating about the person who desired to *kill them.*

☆ ☆ ☆

Peggy Neufeld drifted in and out of consciousness; she was still tied to the ground in the barn. She could hear men talking beside her. Her pain intensified whenever she moved in the slightest. She startled when she felt cold water poured all over her body. She shook her head and tried to open her eyes.

Her naked body started to tremble from the coldness of the water. Her vision slowly returned, and she saw Estrada standing over her. He was undressing as he spoke. "Peggy, you did a bad thing to my friend Roger, and now he wants to kill you. I can help you, and you know it. Just tell us the identity of the woman who saw us, and I will take you to the hospital in Galax."

As she lay there, she knew he would not do as he promised. She looked at him and whispered something. He bent down. "What did you say? I couldn't hear you."

Peggy Neufeld summoned what strength she had left and blurted, "Your mother is a whore!"

Estrada straightened. "OK, have it your way. 'Cause we are going to have it our way." He motioned to Medina. "Roger, she is all yours."

In a quick motion, Medina slapped her and began to caress her from head to toe. He soon was aroused and began to have his way with her.

Peggy closed her eyes and took her mind to a faraway place. She never felt each of the three other men who raped her. When they were finished, Estrada motioned to Medina to bring it to an end. Medina smiled as he took out his knife and slowly slit her throat. He watched as the life seeped from her body.

After Esquivel and Solis left for the house, Estrada took Medina's knife and began carving letters on her chest. Medina laughed when Estrada was finished. He was about to say something, but he caught sight of a face looking at them through a window. "Duke, look! Someone is watching us, and I swear it looked like that old, crazy mountain woman!"

They both ran out the side door and circled the barn. There was no one there. After a second time around, they went back inside. Estrada gave Medina a questioning look.

"Hey, my compadre," said Medina, "I know what I saw, and it was the crazy ole bitch. We need to go up the other side of the mountain and kill her—once and for all!"

"Calm yourself, Roger. That ole woman can do us no harm. We have bigger fish to fry. Stop worrying about her, and help me get the big bag."

Medina shook his head as he went to get the large body bag from the storage bin in the bed of the truck.

Within a half hour, they were driving on the back roads to Hillsville. It was now two o'clock in the morning, and the roads were empty. Estrada stopped his truck a block from the Pantry. They sat in the truck until they were sure it was safe to move about.

In no time, they had placed the body bag on the front steps of the old courthouse on Main Street in Hillsville. They quickly removed Peggy from the bag and laid her on the middle of the deck. Without wasting a moment, they were back in the truck and driving away. No one saw them.

Within fifteen minutes, they were safely back in the compound. Estrada drove the truck into the barn and closed the door. Medina looked at him after he turned off the ignition. "So, what now, Duke? What do we do next?"

Estrada looked at Medina. "We will now decide who *will die next*!"

* * *

Quinn slowly swung his legs over his side of the bed and planted them firmly on the floor. He shook his head and tried to focus on the beautiful sunrise coming up and over the eastern slope.

He tiptoed into the bathroom and gazed into the mirror. "Well," he muttered to himself, "time to pay the price for all that red wine last night!"

He smiled as he tried to push a comb through the unruly forest on his head. While he didn't mind the extra bottles of wine J. W. had gifted them last night, he just regretted Louisa luring him into the hot tub with that last bottle, which had done them in.

As soon as he finished brushing his teeth, he opened the bathroom door. He found Louisa lying on her back in the middle of the bed, and she was snoring louder than he thought humanly possible.

In the kitchen, he looked at the Keurig and decided that a much stronger course of action was needed. He opened the bottom cabinet and took out the French press. The basket was soon filled with the strongest Sumatra beans he had.

While the coffee was brewing, he glanced at the clock on the kitchen wall. He was struck with the fact he had slept an extra hour and a half more than he usually did. As he glanced around the kitchen, the many reasons for his nocturnal bliss were soon apparent.

He counted three empty wine bottles scattered around the room. He managed a halfhearted laugh on his way to the recycle box. The intense smell of the Sumatra brew began to permeate the kitchen.

Just as he began to pour his first cup, Louisa called from the bedroom. "It's all your fault! You scoundrel! Why did you force me to drink all that damn red wine! I feel like a piece of crap! And I can smell that Sumatra you've got going, so your next move better be to bring me a cup of it!"

Quinn laughed and slowly pushed open the bedroom door. "Oh my. Look at you all wrapped up in those sheets and blankets. Guess someone was a bad girl last night. Let's see now. Maybe we need more light in the bedroom."

"McSpain, you had better not open all those drapes! I'll need my sunglasses if you do."

Quinn sat beside her and held out her cup of coffee. She slowly reached out for it, peeking with only one eye open. Quinn pulled it back when it was within inches of her reach.

"Now," she muttered, "you're not being nice to Louisa, and there will be a steep price to pay for that, big man!" Her voice was somewhat muffled by a pillow covering her mouth.

He gently slid the cup into her hand and closed her fingers around it. She held it for a moment, and then she pivoted on her opposite elbow and pulled herself up against the headboard—all without spilling a drop of coffee.

Quinn tried to suppress his laughter. He had never seen her long auburn hair in such a state. He smiled as she took her fist few sips. She frowned as she lifted her eyes from the cup to his. "McSpain, you do know I love you unconditionally, to the end of the universe, but if you love me as much, you will *never* let me drink as much red wine as I did last night!"

He lifted his cup to his lips and enjoyed the coffee's bold taste. "My dearest, do I sense your legendary ability to swill vast amounts of the fruit of the vine is now dissolving because of your…well…advanced age?"

Without a word, she slowly pivoted again, rolled onto her stomach, and propped her head up with pillows. After another sip of coffee, she whispered, "Two things, McSpain. First, kiss my ass; second, be a dear and go down and fire up the hot tub for me. After this coffee, I'm gonna need a good soak. Oh, wait. Third, do make sure someone isn't down there waiting to kill me! *Capisce*?"

Quinn paused for only a slight moment, and then he leaned over and planted two kisses on her creamy-white buttocks. Just as he did, he heard a slight hiss. His reaction was too slow. He could not escape the pungent aroma that permeated his nostrils.

His retreat from the bedroom was followed by rolls of laughter coming from Louisa. Quinn never said a word as he set off to the lower deck to set the heater on the hot tub. He laughed all the way back up the stairs to the kitchen, where he poured himself another cup of coffee.

While he sipped his brew, he picked up his cell phone and punched in the sheriff's number. Leroy answered on the second ring. "Well, I was anxious to get a call from you, Quinn. Are you both OK this morning?"

"Leroy, other than a bad hangover and an odorous and gassy sneak attack, I'm doing fine. What is your schedule like this morning? Time for me?"

"Perfect timing, my friend. I'm open for the next hour and a half. Does that work for you?"

"I'll be at your office in thirty minutes. Get the coffeepot going! Bye."

Quinn walked back to the bedroom and heard Louisa in the shower. He dressed quickly and poked his head into the shower. Louisa turned and stopped washing her belly. She giggled as she smiled at him.

"Take all the time you need to wash up really well, Ms. Hawke, because the Environmental Protection Agency will be here shortly to deal with the mysterious gas leak. In the meantime, I'm off to see Leroy at his office. And I'm happy you're washing up before you get in the hot tub. Hate for you to contaminate the water!"

He slowly closed the shower door, but he saw Louisa begin to gently massage her breasts while closing her eyes and licking her lips. She never said a word.

Quinn drove through the back roads of Carroll County to the sheriff's department. His love for Louisa knew no bounds, and he knew he was blessed to have her in his life. However, the hard reality that someone was trying to kill them was more than a bit disconcerting.

Once inside the sheriff's department, he waved to Levi Blackburn, who was talking on the phone. The sheriff saw

Quinn in the corridor and waved him in. "Now, Quinn McSpain, it has been a bit since you graced us with your presence."

"Well, Leroy, as much as I love you, my friend, I try to maintain my focus on retirement and my unending search for great wine. In that regard, I must pass along that Louisa and I traveled down the mountain yesterday and stopped at the JOLO vineyard on Pilot Mountain. Very impressive, my friend. Very impressive indeed. Wonderful new wines and a chef who knows how to prepare some mighty impressive offerings."

Leroy raised both hands and looked at Quinn with a quizzical look. "So, do tell me whether they have any tables for four people down there. You know Laneisha and I love to try out new places, don't you?"

Quinn held up his right hand. "Stop right there, my friend. After all Louisa has been through lately, I decided we needed some quiet time together. Otherwise, you know I would have called and invited you two to join us. Plus, I know you would have stuck me with the bill!"

Leroy laughed. "So, how is she doing, Quinn?"

"Hey, she is chomping at the bit to find out who has it in for us. We know our mad priest had a lot of personal friends. Or the attacker might be connected to Sally Barber. Or someone from Louisa's FBI past might have a grudge against us."

Before the sheriff could answer, Levi swung the door open to the office and said, "Boss, we just got a call from somebody on Main Street. They discovered a body on the front steps of the old courthouse. They are pretty sure it's Peggy Neufeld."

Both the sheriff and Quinn stood. Leroy grabbed his hat and jacket and looked at Quinn. "Let's go. We can walk. Levi, call Dr. Kahn and have him meet us there as soon as possible."

Within two minutes, they arrived at the front of the old courthouse. The first deputies to arrive had blocked off access and strung police tape around the outer perimeter, next to the street. Deputy Sue Ann Kollman was standing on the top of the steps, and she greeted the sheriff and Quinn after they climbed up the stairs. "Sheriff," she said, "this is just awful. I'm sure this is Peggy Neufeld. I've eaten at the Pantry enough to know who she is. This is awful!"

The sheriff moved past Deputy Kollman and looked down at the bloodstained body, which was mostly covered by the bag. He looked to his side to see Dr. Kahn and Levi walking across the steps. Upon reaching the top of the stairs, Dr. Kahn knelt and slowly opened the rest of the bag.

Leroy cringed as he regarded Peggy's bloodied and beaten face. Her left eye barely hung in its socket. Her arms and hands were badly bruised and probably broken. Dr. Kahn stopped opening the bag when everyone could see the words carved into her breasts and below them.

The only sound came from the trees swaying in the summer breeze. Levi wanted to gag as he read the words to himself. We will find them and kill them.

The sheriff was the first to speak. "Levi, get the state police's crime lab team from Wytheville as soon as you can!"

Levi was on his cell phone before the sheriff finished his sentence. Quinn began to look closely at everything around the steps. After this initial glance, nothing seemed out of place. The sheriff looked at Deputy Kollman and said, "Don't let anyone near these steps!"

The sheriff motioned Levi to follow him, and they headed to the Pantry. Quinn followed a few feet behind. Once inside, he saw Hope Showalter talking to a man he recognized. It was Frank Kauffmann, the pastor at the Mennonite Church.

Pastor Kauffmann looked up when he heard the door close, and he walked over to meet the sheriff. After he shook Leroy's hand, he whispered, "Sheriff, we heard a body was found. Hope opened the Pantry this morning, and someone just came in and told her. Is it Peggy?"

Leroy looked at him. "It is, Pastor."

"Sheriff, we will close the Pantry for the day. As soon as you are available, we need to take Hope to your office because there is something you need to know. I have already called Peggy's parents, and they should be here in no time."

Leroy looked at the pastor. "Do what you can to console Hope and the parents; then take them to my office. I've got to ensure my staff is on top of all this. I will be at my office as soon as I can."

Quinn stood in the background, and he watched what was unfolding in front of him. Leroy turned and looked at Quinn. Just as he did, he saw Samson and Tara Neufeld come in the front door of the Pantry.

Pastor Kauffmann rushed over and took them in his arms. Tara Neufeld sobbed uncontrollably and looked at the sheriff. "Where is my little girl?" she asked.

Pastor Kauffmann held both her shoulders. "Tara, it's not good. You might want to wait—"

She pulled back. "No, I must see her now. No matter what. I need to see her now."

Leroy sucked in a deep breath, walked to her, and took her hand. Samson Neufeld followed them out as they walked to the old courthouse. Dr. Kahn was on his knees examining the body.

After the group climbed the stairs, the doctor looked straight into Tara's eyes and asked her a silent question. She nodded, and tears rolled down her cheeks. The doctor slowly drew back the cloth covering Peggy, exposing just her face and neck. Tara Neufeld felt a chill of horror take hold of her body.

She knelt down and laid her head near her daughter's. Samson held her shoulders as they both sobbed uncontrollably. Tara slowly raised her arms toward the heavens. "Our Lord Jesus, what has happened to her? Why her? Why her?"

Samson slowly lifted his wife to her feet. She wobbled as they headed back to the Pantry.

A crowd was already forming in front of the old courthouse. The last time a killing happened at the courthouse was in March of 1912. At that time, the Allen Clan and local lawmen engaged in an epic gunfight, which made national headlines.

Levi, now standing next to Quinn, watched them, and he wiped the moisture forming in his eyes. He looked at Quinn. "By the grace of God, McSpain, we are going to do whatever it takes to catch the motherfuckers who did this. *No matter what it takes*!"

* * *

Estrada was tired. He, along with Medina, Solis, and Esquivel, had scrubbed and washed every inch of his truck and the barn to erase any trace of Peggy Neufeld. All her clothes and the rags they had used were burned. He couldn't think of anything they might have missed. He also knew he was hungry.

At that very moment, his wife, Elva, walked into the barn. She walked around and looked in the truck. She then stepped into the bathroom. "Did you scrub this room down?" she asked as she came out.

"We did. Yes, we did," Medina replied. "Now, is there some food for us to eat after all this work?" he asked.

Elva walked around some more. "Are you sure there are no traces of her DNA anywhere?"

Medina looked at Estrada and said, "I'm more worried about that crazy witch who looked through the window and saw us do what we were doing. We need to find that crazy woman first and kill her."

Elva walked right over to Medina. "You will do no such thing! That woman has more power than us. Bad things will happen to us if we even try to kill her!"

Estrada stood still for a moment. "Elva, she saw us kill that woman. I don't think she will call the cops or anything, but the real problem is that she might not have liked what we did to that girl."

Esquivel and Solis nodded in agreement.

"So, Duke," said Elva, "what do you think we should do? Maybe we should wait to see if she does anything. Who knows? She might not do a damn thing."

Estrada thought for a moment. "No, we need to deal with this and deal with it right now." He looked at Solis and Esquivel. "Who is willing to take care of this?"

Both men looked at each other. Solis smiled a wicked smile. "I will take care of that old woman. I'm not scared of her."

Esquivel breathed a sigh of relief.

Elva shook her head. "I am telling you this is a bad idea. You just don't understand what we are dealing with here. She is not a normal woman. Her powers are crazy powerful."

Solis walked over and put his arm around Elva. "Not to worry. I'll be safe. I'll have my best friends, Smith and Wesson, with me. They have special powers too. They shoot bullets!"

The men laughed as they walked from the barn to the house for dinner. Elva didn't laugh; she was thinking that her friend Luis Solis was the one more likely *to be killed.*

CHAPTER 16

Tommie Cruz sat at his desk and watched the multiple screens before him. He chuckled at WikiLeaks's disclosures concerning the Clinton campaign. He knew exactly which group of Russian hackers was responsible for the disclosures, which he felt sure would play a huge part in her losing the election.

However, the local news from the *Galax Gazette* caught his immediate attention. The fact that a young Mennonite girl had been found dead in Hillsville just reinforced what he had suspected all along.

He had no doubt the prior murders of the two local drug kingpins were connected to this young woman's death. He realized that it didn't take a genius to understand that someone had witnessed those killings.

He had known for some time that a power play was happening in the drug trade in Southwest Virginia. He also knew that Duke Estrada was at the top of the local totem pole of Hispanic drug dealers. Tommie had set up Estrada's secure network some two years before. Estrada thought it had been done by a network wizard in California, someone hired by his boss in Mexico.

With all that, coupled with the sheriff's investigators looking for whoever had tried to kill Louisa Hawke and Quinn McSpain, Tommie figured the local resources were strained to their limits. However, the fact that Hawke and McSpain had to be more cautious and alert did weigh on what he needed to do next.

He had this thought as he left his office and went to the bathroom. After he had relieved himself, he looked at the back of his head. The wound he had suffered when Hawke hit him on the head with her wine bottle was healing well. The throb he felt now was from the intensity of his desire to kill them.

His iPhone vibrated as he walked back to his office. He looked down and saw Missy's name on the screen. He hadn't seen her since she tended to the back of his skull. She had left Galax to visit her girlfriend in Rodanthe, in the Outer Banks of North Carolina.

He read her text message.

> Do you miss me? 'Cause I miss you, and I mean *all* of you! I'll be back in Galax tomorrow afternoon. Hope we can catch up. See you soon, you big hunk!

He didn't reply until he sat down at his desk. His mind drifted to the several sexual encounters they had enjoyed together. He had to admit she enjoyed sex as much as he did, but she made sure he always had a good time.

He typed his reply.

> Baby, see you tomorrow! Call me when you get in.

After he sent the message, his smile changed to a grin because he knew her time as his sexual partner could not go on forever. Despite the detail he had put into his precautions, Missy's closeness to him would always be a liability. He just didn't know when he would *kill her.*

☆ ☆ ☆

Leroy Jefferson sat back in his office chair and rubbed his temples. He had come back to the station with Levi and Quinn after dealing with the morbid discovery at the old courthouse. The image of Peggy Neufeld lying on the steps made him sick to his stomach. There were no words to describe his disgust.

He looked up as Levi and Quinn entered his office with fresh cups of coffee. Quinn slid one of the cups over to Leroy. No one spoke as they took sips of the fresh brew. The quiet, however, was short lived. The intercom line on the sheriff's desk buzzed.

Leroy put his phone to his ear and listened to the lobby receptionist tell him Pastor Frank Kauffmann, his wife, and Hope Showalter had just arrived. "Bring them on up, please" Leroy said, and he hung up. "The good pastor, his wife, and

Hope Showalter are here to see us," he said to Levi and Quinn, and he put his coffee down.

Quinn stood. "Should I leave you two alone with them?" he asked.

The sheriff motioned him to sit. "No, Quinn. I want you to hear what they have to say. You might just catch something we miss."

As soon as he said that, the door to his office opened, and Pastor Kauffmann poked his head in. "Is this a good time, Sheriff?"

Leroy stood and went to the door. "Come in. Sit. This is the time we all need to find out exactly what is going on."

Quinn moved to the couch, and Levi moved one more chair in front of the sheriff's desk, providing three in total. Before everyone sat, the sheriff said, "I'm not sure if you know my senior investigator, Levi Blackburn."

Levi came forward and shook their hands.

The sheriff pointed to Quinn and said, "This is Quinn McSpain. He has helped us on several other serious matters in the county. Some time back, he was instrumental in the capture of a crazy Catholic priest who had been terrorizing our community."

Quinn stepped forward and shook their hands before sitting back on the couch.

After the pastor, his wife, and Hope Showalter sat, Leroy paused for a moment before he spoke. "Can I get anyone anything to drink before we begin?"

No one responded.

The pastor spoke first. "Sheriff, shortly after the killing of the two men in the alley, Hope came to see me and Stella. What she told us was frightening. We have been trying to decide what to do about it. Until now. The killing of Peggy Neufeld has scared us to the core. We just don't know what to do, and we sorely need your help. So, Hope, I guess the best way to begin is to tell the sheriff what you need to tell him."

All eyes focused on Hope. She rubbed her hands together for several moments before she said, "Sheriff, I apologize for not talking to you sooner. I realize I should have talked with you when we spoke in the Pantry. I guess I was too terrified to say anything that day. Well, with what happened to Peggy, I am frightened for my life and my daughter's life." She stopped for a moment to wipe tears from her eyes. "Sheriff, I was there at the Pantry the night those poor men were killed. I had gone home to Volunteer Gap after I closed that night, but I forgot the cashbox at the Pantry. So, I returned with my daughter, Hannah. She went to the back deck, and I checked the phone for messages and gathered the cashbox.

"After I finished, I went to the deck to get Hannah. What I saw, Sheriff, was purely out of hell. I held Hannah close and tried to shield her from seeing that the men in the alley had just cut off the heads of two men, whose bodies were lying on the ground. For a moment, I was too petrified to even move a muscle. I just trembled with fear.

"Just as I saw one of the men see us, I turned, took Hannah's hand, and ran back into the Pantry. I locked the back door behind us and quickly ran to the front door. I looked out the front window and saw one of your deputies driving past on Court Street.

"I didn't waste any time getting Hannah into my van. As I drove off, I looked back into the alley but didn't see anyone there. I think they might have seen the deputy's car as well. As I dove back to Volunteer Gap, I checked my side mirrors to see if we were being followed. I don't think we were." She stopped speaking and glanced at Kauffmann.

"Hope," said Kauffmann, "came to me soon after and told me what had happened. I also know I should have come to you sooner. The killing of Peggy Neufeld, which has frightened me to my roots, has forced us to give up our reticence. I'm now convinced these killers will stop at nothing to find Hope and Hannah and *kill them*!"

☆ ☆ ☆

Luis Solis took the last sip of his morning coffee. He smiled as he took out his Glock 30 pistol. He checked the magazine and counted ten bullets for the .45 ACP. He thought about taking more ammunition but resisted the urge because the target was an old, unarmed woman.

After holstering the pistol, he walked toward the back door, where Estrada was coming in from the barn. Estrada took Solis by the shoulders and said, "Happy hunting, my friend. I'm betting you'll be back before dinner tonight."

Solis laughed and said, "My friend, I hope I can be back for a late lunch."

He then walked to the entrance of the compound, clicked on the gate opener in his pocket, and watched the massive security gate open. After crossing the bridge, he closed the gate and crossed the dirt road.

He stopped at the edge of the forest and regarded the steep incline. He looked in the general direction of where he had seen smoke rise in the past. He unsheathed his machete and started to whack away at the thorny underbrush that came across his path.

Within a half hour or so, he realized the incline was much steeper than he had expected. He paused and sat for a moment to catch his breath. He popped the top off his canteen. He needed to quench his thirst.

As he did so, his presence was felt several hundred feet above, in a small cabin perched on a cliff. Inside, an older woman sat on a wooden chair. She was stirring the remnants of black tea and coffee grounds in the bottom of a porcelain cup. Tiller, as she was known to few, smiled as she closed her eyes and saw the image of someone sitting on a rock far below.

She was not surprised. She knew it was only a matter of time before the unholy men who had tortured that poor girl would come looking for her. It mattered not. She never feared bad people. She understood that her powers came from the Appalachian queens who had come before her.

They were daughters of Celts and the offspring of Druids and medieval mavens. The blood in her veins was laced with old magic and secrets long buried in the heirloom hills, in which she traveled. She stood and stretched her six-foot-plus frame and spit out the rancid juice from the cud of tobacco in her cheek. Her black cat jumped out of range of the juice and hissed up a storm but never dropped the dead rat it was feasting on.

No, she was not frightened.

Solis got up from the rock he was sitting on and started up what he thought was a small path heading up the mountainside. His steps became smaller as the incline grew steeper. He squinted and looked into the sunshine spilling over the top of the ridge. Turkey buzzards were circling in the thermals high above.

He chuckled to himself, imagining the buzzards' delight when he would leave the old witch's dead body for them to feast on, but a noise he heard brought his focus back to the path before him. It was the sound of something like sticks pounding on a bench, but he wasn't sure.

As he climbed, the noise was getting closer and closer. Within a few minutes, he was looking over the final ridge and scrutinizing a dilapidated cabin that was no more than a hundred yards from where he was crouching. His right hand slipped the snap off his holster. He wrapped his fingers around the grip and slowly pulled it out.

There was no smoke coming from the small and crooked chimney. The front door to the cabin was open. A rocking chair was on the little porch. No one was in it, but it was rocking back and forth on its own.

Though Solis was not a superstitious person, everything he noticed was causing him to sweat. He tightened his grip on his Glock and inched forward, trying to prevent any sharp noises. Within a few minutes, he was within fifty feet of the porch.

His heart pounded quickly when he heard someone humming a tune from within the cabin. He had never heard anything quite like it before. A chill ran up his spine. He slowly and quietly crept onto the porch. He peered into the only window but couldn't see a thing.

In one leap, he bounded through the front door. His pointed his pistol straight ahead. He sensed movement to his left, where he aimed and fired a round. The sound of the .45 ACP was deafening inside the small cabin. The slug hit a chair immediately in front of him, barely missing the black cat that bounded out of the way.

Solis took everything he could see into his mental inventory. The one-room interior was sparse—only a small bunk bed in the corner and a potbelly stove in the other corner. He knew the witch was not in the cabin.

In two hops, the cat was out the front door, and Solis turned to watch it head straight to a tall, thick pine some fifteen feet from the cabin door. He spun around as soon as he realized the old woman was standing in front of the tree in full sight.

He quickly took aim with the Glock at the woman. As soon as the bullet left the chamber, the woman vanished. He fired again but futilely. Solis bounded onto the porch and looked in every direction. He caught a glimpse of her standing in front of a massive oak tree in the opposite direction.

Another two rounds burst from his pistol. In the milliseconds before the slugs reached the oak tree, the woman vanished again. He spun around to see her sitting about ten feet away. She was now on the ground by a smaller tree, which was close to the cabin.

He believed his aim was true when he squeezed off his next-to-last round. The slug shattered the branch but couldn't hit what wasn't there. He cussed, spinning around and hoping to catch another glimpse of her.

On the other side of the cabin, he saw her standing between two pines joined at the base. He ran forward and fired off his last round. It hit the tree on the left and nothing else. Solis was quivering. He put the pistol back into the holster and slid his hunting knife from its sheath.

He heard the black cat scratching at the base of the massive oak tree. He sensed his prey was behind that tree. "I'm going to kill you, old lady, and I'm not scared of you one bit.

You might have dodged those bullets, but I'm going to cut you with my knife."

Solis inched forward toward the oak tree. Tiller smiled from behind the tree and loosened the rawhide lace that held a small pouch hanging below her throat. She loosened the top and gently shook the contents in the pouch.

Solis held his knife up as he started to come around the left side of the tree. She knew exactly where he was. She was watching him through the eyes *of her cat.*

CHAPTER 17

Quinn gripped the steering wheel as he drove home from the sheriff's department. The image of Peggy Neufeld lying on that deck kept flashing through his mind. He hoped and prayed Hope and Hannah Showalter would recognize someone from the pictures they now were looking at, which had been provided by the state police and the sheriff's department.

However, he wasn't so sure they would recognize and confirm any identification at all. He understood that darkness had been setting in that night, and both Hope and Hannah were in shock. Moreover, they witnessed the killings several weeks ago, and that lapse would further hinder the process of identifying suspects. That interval, in itself, could change what they actually witnessed into something they *thought* they had seen.

As he walked into the house, he could smell the soup cooking on the stove. He went over, tipped the lid, and confirmed what he had thought: the pea soup would soon be ready.

"Hey, McSpain, back away from that soup, and come here."

Quinn walked into the front study, where Louisa was at her desk. She was looking at her computer screen. She swiveled and looked at him. "OK, spill the beans. What did you find out at the sheriff's?"

Quinn sat in the chair near her desk and took her hands. He took her through the horrific discovery of Peggy Neufeld's body, as well as Pastor Kauffmann and Hope's visit to the sheriff's office. Louisa winced when Quinn finished telling her what had happened.

"Jesus, Quinn, what in God's name is happening here? My gut feeling is that the killers know they were seen, but they don't seem to know exactly who saw them. The problem with that is there are just so many Mennonite women who work at the Pantry!"

Quinn sat back and looked at her. "That is exactly the problem. As they go through the process of elimination, more and more young, innocent women might die. Hope and Hannah are now with Levi and the state police. They're looking at pictures of all the Hispanic drug players from the surrounding counties, as well as the border counties in North Carolina.

"We should know shortly if they make a positive identification of any of the possible suspects. We gotta realize that both were pretty shook up that night. I just hope Leroy and his troops get lucky and get a hit on whoever is responsible."

Louisa nodded and picked up a notepad from the side of her computer. "So, while you were gone, I traded e-mails with Jay Fisher. Who is Jay Fisher? Well, he is the owner and designer of the famous Flamesteed knives. I sent him a picture of the particular knife that almost killed me, and he had a lot to say.

"He recalled that knife rather well. According to Fisher, the buyer was a real prick during the whole process. He took forever before finally being satisfied with the final knife design. Fisher was surprised the buyer never balked at the price tag of eight thousand dollars.

"So, I asked Fisher if he had any idea who the buyer was. He laughed before he answered. Fisher claimed he tried to find out who owned the buyer's telephone. Turns out the buyer used a different burner phone for all of their seven conversations.

"What is more, Fisher was surprised that the payment for the knife came in the mail. The small box he received contained eight thousand dollars in cash. The box was postmarked somewhere in Florida and didn't have a return address.

"The real kicker was that the buyer instructed Fisher to mail the knife to a post-office box in Winston-Salem. Fisher did as he was instructed and never heard back from the buyer—in any way, shape, or form."

After listening to Louisa, Quinn scratched his head for a moment. "Jeez, Louisa, it sounds as if Fisher tried his hardest to find out exactly who the buyer was."

"Quinn, Fisher told me that many of his buyers are a bit secretive, but he said this guy was the very best at protecting his identity. Oh, I almost forgot, Fisher also tried to trace the buyer's e-mail address. Even went so far as to have a geeky computer friend of his try to get a bead on the buyer. Didn't work. His friend struck out on all attempts to trace the origin of the e-mails. He claimed the buyer was hidden under more layers than a Duncan Hines layer cake."

Quinn stood and started to pace around the room. "So, what we've got is just about nothing. No prints on a knife that was purchased in almost absolute secrecy. The closest lead we have is a post-office box in Winston-Salem, and even that could be a diversion."

Before he could continue, Louisa handed him her notebook and pointed out an entry. Quinn smiled and said, "So, we have the number of a post-office box to work with. I can reach out to Bruce Sprinkle, the postal inspector in Greensboro. He might be able to help us with this."

Louisa looked at him. "Wasn't Sprinkle the inspector who helped you put the cotton buyer that worked for the underwear company in prison for six years?"

"Yes, the one and only. A very good investigator. We knew that rascal had received over two million dollars in kickbacks, and Sprinkle helped me prove it. Ah, how I sometimes miss my corporate life!"

Louisa bent over in laughter. "Big man, while you were one of the best in the business world, I know darn well you wouldn't trade what we have now for anything! Would you?"

Quinn took her into his arms. "Ms. Hawke, you make every day worth living. I wouldn't trade this for...well, maybe a few moments with Libby!"

With that, he dropped, pivoted, and ran toward the bedroom. Louisa was in hot pursuit, and she tackled him onto their bed. They rolled around and laughed. Louisa pulled his sweat shirt off with one hand, and then she pulled her top off. Their passion grew in a flash as they entwined themselves and became one. She felt the swelling of their shared desire.

Quinn was the first to lie still; he cocked an ear up. "Did you hear that?" he asked.

Louisa slipped off the side of the bed and opened the dresser by her. She took her pistol out and slowly peered out the side window. Her pistol was at the ready.

"Oh my God," she whispered, causing Quinn to tense up. "Are you expecting a UPS delivery?"

"No, but did you know his name is George?" Quinn said, and he giggled.

"How do you know that?" she asked.

At that moment, their laughter could be heard *for miles.*

☆ ☆ ☆

Levi Blackburn was pleased that Jeannie Wishart from the DEA was going to join him while Hope and Hannah looked at the mug shots of the known Hispanic drug dealers in the area. While he was still romantically involved with his girlfriend at the time, he believed he would happily visit Wishart on the side.

Just as soon as he smiled that thought away, Wishart entered the conference room that had been set for them to use. He stood as she came to him and gave him a hug.

"Now, Levi Blackburn, don't you just smell like a man on a mission?" Levi blushed, and she sat down and smiled. "OK," she said, "let's get down to business. I'm appalled at what happened to Peggy Neufeld. Listen, there is little doubt Felix Estrada and his motley crew were responsible for this. All we need is for them to point their fingers at the right ones."

Just as she finished talking, the conference room door opened, and the sheriff walked in. Hope and Hannah Showalter followed. Leroy introduced them to Wishart after they sat down. He was pleased a woman would be taking them through the process of looking at the mug shots.

Wishart smiled at Hope and Hannah, and she moved her chair closer to where they sat. Levi understood she was eliminating space between her and the Showalters. Wishart then took and held Hope's hand and said, "Hope, please understand that I know the fear and stress you both are feeling. You have been through a living hell, and it isn't getting any better. You have my word that I will do all I can to protect you from any harm.

"You are doing the right thing by being here and trying to identify those responsible. I have some twenty pictures you will look at. I know it was dark and scary that night when you saw what happened, so take your time as you look at these pictures. If you see anyone who resembles either of the men you saw, put that picture to the right side. If there is no resemblance at all, put the picture on the left side. Do you have any questions?"

Hope and Hannah looked at each other and shook their heads.

"OK, let's begin," said Wishart, slowly passing the first picture to Hope.

Hope looked at it, and then she showed it to Hannah. "No, Mamma," Hannah said.

Hope placed the picture on the left side.

Within five minutes, Hope and Hannah had looked at all the pictures. Only five were on the right side. Wishart put the other pictures back into her folder. She stood and looked at the five selected pictures. The pictures of Duke Estrada, Roger Medina, Solis, and Esquivel stared back at her. The fifth picture belonged to a Hispanic undercover DEA agent she had thrown into the mix. He bore a strong resemblance to Estrada.

Wishart looked at them both. She picked up Estrada's picture. "Are you positive this man was in the alley that night?"

Hope looked at Hannah before she spoke. "Ms. Wishart, I am not one hundred percent sure. It might be him, but it also could be that other man." She pointed to the DEA agent's picture. "It was so dark, and I was so frightened by it all. Hannah, what do you think, my child?"

Hannah stood and took a closer look at both pictures. "Mother, I'm not sure. Both of those men look alike."

"Take your time, and look at the other three men as well," Wishart said.

Both Hope and Hannah stood and closely examined the pictures. They spoke to each other as they did. Hope picked up Medina's picture and looked at Wishart. "We are probably ninety percent sure this man was in the alley. But certainly not one hundred percent."

Wishart looked at Levi and the sheriff. She then smiled at Hope and Hannah. "You have done a great job with this. We now have more to work with as we move forward, but rest assured that all of us in law enforcement are doing our best to catch these killers."

She hugged both of them before the sheriff led them out of the conference room. After the door was closed, she sat down and looked at Levi. "So, what do you think, Blackburn? Enough here to bring the case before a grand jury?"

Levi looked at her for a long moment, and then the sheriff came back into the conference room. "Jeannie," said Levi, "I believe we are on shaky ground with what we just saw. Hell, they 'bout pointed out your undercover DEA guy. They were shook up pretty bad that night, and it was dark." Levi turned to the sheriff. "What do you think?"

Leroy stood and walked to the window, looking out and thinking. He turned back to them. "Let me suggest something. If this goes to court, Estrada and his friends will be lawyered up with the best money can buy in Virginia. Hope and poor Hannah will be torn to shreds unless they are one hundred percent positive with their identifications.

"We don't have any physical evidence linking Estrada and his gang to either of the murders. We know darn well they were responsible, but we need more to tie it all together. But, undoubtedly, they will continue in their grizzly efforts to find out who saw them that night.

"Levi, run over to the courthouse and find some time with Judge Turner. See what he thinks about all this. Jeannie, I have put deputies on Hope's home in Volunteer Gap. They will never be alone. Now, I need some help here watching Estrada and what they get up to."

Wishart stood, closed her briefcase, and looked at Leroy. "Sheriff, we will give you all the resources we have, and I will coordinate with the state police to get whatever help they can provide."

At that moment, the sheriff's cell phone rang. He saw Pastor Kauffmann's name on the screen. "Hello, Pastor. What can I help you with?"

Leroy talked on his phone for several minutes.

When the call was finished, the sheriff said, "It seems as if Pastor Kauffmann has already met with Hope, and they want to meet with me as soon as they can. It seems they have their own plan as to *what needs to be done.*"

☆ ☆ ☆

Tiller looked down at Solis squirming on the ground in front of her. She had stuffed a rag in his mouth to muffle his screams. She screwed back on the top of the small vial that hung from her neck.

The contents had worked to perfection. Solis's eyeballs were slowly dissolving. She smiled as she tied his hands tightly to his belt. The smell of his urine permeated the air from his damp blue jeans.

As the day slowly ended, she slowly dragged Solis down the mountain trail. His muffled screams became weaker and weaker. At an hour before sunset, she reached the bottom of the hill. She saw all the trucks were parked close to the barn.

With a flick of her wrist, she cut the rope from his wrists and made him stand against the front gate. She then took the rag from his mouth and dropped it to the ground.

Solis, barely in a conscious state, could feel the bars of the iron gate. He knew he was in front of the compound. He sucked in as much air as he could and let out a primal scream. The effort weakened him and forced him to cling to the gate.

Elva Estrada was in the kitchen. She was enjoying the late-evening breeze floating through the window. She was startled when she heard a strange sound coming from the front of the house. In a moment, she was at the front window and was looking through her binoculars.

She shuddered and ran from the house to the barn to get Estrada and Medina. Before she got there, both emerged from the barn door. "Come quickly! I think Luis is at the front gate!" she yelled.

Both drew their weapons from their belt holsters, and they ran toward the gate. Estrada was the first to arrive. He entered the code to open the gate. By then, Solis had fallen to the ground.

Solis was lying facedown on the ground and twitching uncontrollably. Estrada went to his knees and gently rolled him over. Within a moment, he could feel the bile coming up his esophageal tube. He focused on Solis and saw two empty sockets where his eyes belonged.

Medina gagged as he looked at Solis. Estrada placed his arms under Solis's armpits and signaled Medina to take his legs. Elva cried uncontrollably as they headed to the barn. Once inside, they placed Solis on a bed in the barn's back bedroom.

By then, Esquivel had come running from the house. He shrieked in horror when he saw Solis on the bed. Estrada put his ear to Solis's mouth, thinking he had heard him try to utter something. He listened for a moment and then straightened.

Elva looked at him. "Did he say anything?"

Estrada frowned for a moment. "Yes, he did. He said to kill him."

Elva backed away from the bed. Tears streamed down her cheeks. "My God, I told him not to go!"

Esquivel looked at Estrada. "Duke, we have to kill that witch! I will kill her myself!"

"You will do no such thing, Tony. Elva is right. That woman has more powers than we can imagine. We must leave her alone and deal with the other mess we have on our hands right now."

Elva looked at him. "So, what do we do with Luis? Do we take him to the hospital in Galax or what?"

"No, Elva, we shall do no such thing. We can only *honor his last wish.*"

☼ ☼ ☼

Missy was glad to be back from her trip to the Outer Banks. She had enjoyed the time with her friend Claire, who lived there, but she had been disappointed in the slim pickings of beach-boys. While some seemed buff and fit enough to gain her interest, most were no smarter than the surfboards they so loved.

She did have a brief moment with a young ship captain. He had the curliest blond hair she had ever seen and a chiseled body to boot. However, she kept thinking of Tommie, who was back in Galax, and the places he could take her to.

The six-hour ride back to Virginia seemed to take forever as she snaked her way through the traffic in North Carolina. It was almost four thirty in the afternoon when she arrived at her apartment. She quickly unpacked and threw a few things into the washer.

After a quick shower, she admired her lithe and tan body in the mirror. Her tan was extra even because she had spent most of her time on the nude beach at Rodanthe. She felt a twinge of excitement as she rubbed moisturizer over her ample breasts and squeezed her nipples.

She was soon thinking of Tommie and what she needed from him. For a moment, that thought dissipated as she dressed. After buttoning her halter top, she headed out the door and over to Tommie's house.

She knocked on the door and then pushed the bell button. Several minutes passed without any response from inside. She knew Tommie had cameras covering every possible entry of his house. In the next moment, she took her phone from her pocket and sent him a text message.

His response was immediate. He was out on business, and he would meet her in an hour at Macado's. She replied with a thumbs-up emoji.

She smiled as she crossed the street and walked into Macado's. She noticed the usual happy-hour crowd had assembled. Jake, the bartender, waved at her as she walked in and sat at the end of the bar.

"Well, Missy, where in tarnation have you been? I've missed looking at your beautiful face for a couple of weeks now," Jake said.

Without hesitating, Missy said, "You missed looking at my boobs, you dirty old man."

Jake broke out in laughter as he poured her a draft beer. "I must admit you add a certain something to the atmosphere."

"Indeed, she does," said a man, and he slid onto the barstool beside her.

Missy looked to her side and recognized Bradford Frank, who was a young editor at the *Galax Gazette.* Missy liked Brad because he was intelligent and didn't get consumed with thinking about how he could get into her pants. "So, my dear Brad, you do like looking at my womanhood, don't you?" she asked with a sultry smile.

"Missy, I am a man. However, I'm a happily married man. One who doesn't cheat on the woman he loves. If I did, though, rest assured you would be my very first pick!"

Both Missy and Jake started to laugh. Brad took a sip of beer. After Missy stopped laughing, she looked at Brad and said, "So, what have I missed in this grand metropolitan area during the past couple of weeks?"

"Well, let's see. Where do I begin? I'm sure you know about the two drug dealers beheaded in the alley behind the Pantry. The situation has become a lot more interesting. A young Mennonite woman was found dead on the steps of the old courthouse just a day ago."

"Jeez, Brad, that is terrible! Do the police have any clues?" Missy asked.

"Listen, I attended a press conference the sheriff held. The state police and folks from the DEA were also there. My impression is they might have a few clues, but they don't seem to be sure about who is responsible."

Jake looked at them both. "If you ask me, I bet the Hispanic drug lords are responsible. They want to control all the drug traffic in this area, and there is no better way to get competition out of the way!"

Brad nodded in agreement. He then turned to Missy. "And you probably didn't hear about the attempted murder of Louisa Hawke in Fancy Gap. She is the retired FBI woman who solved the kidnapping and murder done by that crazy priest, with help from her boyfriend, Quinn McSpain. It seems some nut tried to kill her with a knife while she was in her hot tub. Well, the idiot missed her, and she smashed his head with a wine bottle."

Missy focused on Brad and digested what he had just said. "Hey, exactly when did the attack on the FBI woman happen?"

Brad considered her question. "Probably just before you went to the beach."

Her look became intense. "Did they catch the guy?"

Brad shook his head. "No, they didn't. The cops checked all the hospitals in the area. Hell, they even checked the hospitals in Roanoke and Winston-Salem. Nothing."

Missy turned away, closed her eyes, and grew pale. Brad and Jake looked at her. Brad said, "Missy, are you OK?"

A second later, she pivoted off the barstool and headed for the door without saying *another word.*

☆ ☆ ☆

Leroy Jefferson and Levi Blackburn drove toward Pastor Kauffmann's house in silence. Each was digesting all the horrific events that had happened in Carroll County in the past four weeks. Nothing had disturbed this normally peaceful and bucolic part of Southwest Virginia since the demonic priest abducted those two children in the fog.

Leroy looked at Levi. "Did you talk with Judge Turner yet?"

"I did, and he is mighty skeptical about our chances to bring any charges against Estrada and his gang of assholes. He said we need an absolutely certain identification from Hope and Hannah and some strong physical evidence to make a case."

Leroy tightened his grip on the steering wheel as he turned into Pastor Kauffmann's driveway. He waved to the deputy parked near the side of the house. "Levi, we need to do everything we can to put Estrada behind bars. The carnage won't stop until we do!"

Levi nodded in agreement, and he knocked on the front door. Pastor Kauffmann opened the door and led them into the living room. Hope and Hannah were sitting next to Stella, the pastor's wife. Leroy recognized the three other men in the room as senior leaders of the local Mennonite community.

The pastor sat next to the sheriff and said, "Would either of you like some coffee?"

Levi nodded in the affirmative, and the sheriff declined. When Levi had his cup, Pastor Kauffmann said, "Sheriff, we are gravely concerned about the immediate well-being of Hope and Hannah. We all saw what happened to Peggy Neufeld. Now, there is no doubt in anyone's mind that these murderers will stop at nothing to locate Hope and Hannah. While we appreciate that you have a deputy with them, we feel there might be a better solution for their well-being." He paused for a moment before he continued. "We believe Hope and Hannah must be taken to a secret place, one where they will be safe from those who wish to harm them. I have spoken to someone who is willing to help, and I have known this person for many years."

The sheriff and Levi looked at each other before the sheriff spoke. "Pastor, if they leave here, they will lose the protection we can give them. May I ask exactly where you plan to take them?"

Pastor Kauffmann slowly rubbed his hands together. "Sheriff, unbeknown to most travelers in the world, there is a wonderful but isolated Mennonite community in Belize. Its name is Blue Creek, and it is in the northernmost part of the country. Some five hundred members of a tight-knit community live there. I spoke with John, who is both a dear friend of mine and the pastor of the congregation there. I explained what is happening here and the imminent threat to Hope and Hannah. He completely understood and suggested we consider sending Hope and Hannah to Blue Creek for safekeeping."

Levi scratched his head for a moment. "Pastor, pardon me, but don't most folks go to Belize for honeymoons, the beach, and some snorkeling?"

Pastor Kauffmann smiled. "Levi, you are right, but that destination is in the southern part of the country. Blue Creek is a very long and secluded way from all that. The Mennonites in Blue Creek are cattle ranchers and farmers. They even have a cooperative rice mill they operate.

"Sheriff, I have traveled to Blue Creek, and I believe Hope and Hannah would be safe there. Hope and Hannah would blend in well there, and the safety they would have would allow ample time for the murderers here in Carroll County to be found and brought to justice."

The room was quiet as the sheriff looked around. "Pastor, let me assure you that the well-being of Hope and Hannah is my highest priority, but what you're suggesting begets a whole host of other questions: How will they get there? Should someone accompany them on the trip? Who will know where they are? These are but a few of the questions and concerns I have with all this."

Pastor Kauffmann looked at him. "Sheriff, rest assured that no one outside this room will know where they are. We understand the importance of maintaining secrecy with all this. After all, two lives are at stake here."

The sheriff was taken with an idea that was suddenly forming in his mind. He looked at Pastor Kauffmann and said, "I think I might have a path forward with all this. Let me quickly check out the possibilities, and I promise to get back to you before the end of the day."

He stood and shook hands with everyone before leaving. He also hugged Hope and Hannah. Levi followed him to their car. Once they were on the highway, Levi said, "OK, don't keep me in the dark. What kind of plan are you thinking about, and where are we going?"

The sheriff looked straight ahead and *didn't say a word.*

☆ ☆ ☆

Elva cried as Estrada and Medina looked at Solis on the bed. He was barely breathing. Elva asked, "What are you going to do with him?"

"Elva, go to the house. We will do what needs to be done. Do not let Maria come out here and see us. Now go!"

Elva pounded on his chest with her fists, and tears streamed down her cheeks. She turned and ran to the house. As she approached the house, Maria came out the door and started for the barn. Elva stopped her and pulled her toward the house. Maria screamed, "Do not kill him! Do not kill him!"

Estrada looked at Medina and said, "Go to the side of the barn and start a fire in a large barrel. Then come back inside."

Medina nodded, and he grabbed a gas can by the door as he left.

Estrada sat on the chair near the bed and could hear faint breaths coming from Solis. "My brother, we have traveled many good miles together. You have been a good friend and have saved my ass many times. Today, though, I must send you to the next life. I think you believe in heaven and God. You have lived well, my friend."

Solis coughed, and blood dripped from the side of his mouth. Medina leaned even closer. He thought Solis was trying to speak. Solis only said, "Kill me. I'm going to hell."

Estrada closed his eyes. He held Solis's throat with his right hand and slowly squeezed it closed. Solis barely shook when he took his last breath. Estrada stood when Medina came back and stood beside him.

"Is he dead?" Medina asked.

"Yes. He was our friend, and now we must do what needs to be done."

Medina nodded in agreement and went inside the storage room; he returned with two axes and a two-man saw.

For the next thirty minutes, both men cut Solis into pieces that would fit into the large fire barrel. When they were finished, they stood by the barrel and watched the final pieces of their friend turn to ashes.

Estrada then turned and went back into the barn, and Medina was close behind him. Inside, they sat at the round table. Medina was the first to speak. "So, what is our next step, Duke?"

Estrada rubbed his temples with both hands before speaking. "Roger, I believe we have made an impression on those religious people and, of course, the police. They understand we are trying real hard to find out who saw us that night. If I were one of the witnesses, I would be real scared right now. I think they are probably going to try to hide that woman and her little girl. I know I would if someone wanted to kill my wife and kid.

"Plus, the police will try to protect them as well. And don't forget that the sheriff's people will be helped by the state police—those fuckers! The assholes from the DEA will be in on it too. I think the religious people might trust their own kind before they trust the police, though.

"So, my friend, I suggest we lie low for a while since the cops will be watching us. Now, I know they don't have enough evidence to arrest us. If they did, we would be in jail.

"After things cool off a bit, we will go and talk to the person who is in charge of their church. I bet he or she will know exactly whom we are looking for and where we might find them. I would be very surprised if their head honcho isn't clued in on what we need to know."

Medina smiled as he looked at Estrada. "You, my friend, are a smart man, but I am worried about the police. They will be watching our every move. We must be very careful."

"My friend, do not worry. We will not be killing anyone… *at least, not for a while.*"

CHAPTER 18

It didn't take long for Levi to figure out where the sheriff was going. As soon as Leroy turned off the dirt road and headed up the curving hill, they both could see Quinn's house on the top of the cliff. Leroy was pleased to see both Louisa's Volvo and Quinn's truck in the driveway.

Quinn was the first to hear the car coming up the driveway. He came out on the porch and smiled when he saw the sheriff and Levi get out of the car. "Well," he said, "pray tell. To what do we owe the pleasure of a visit from Carroll County's finest?"

Levi laughed. "McSpain, it just must be your lucky day. We know you might need some protection from that beautiful woman who shares your space."

As he finished, Louisa walked out on the porch. "Oh my God, Quinn, let's get back in the house and lock the door! When these two show up unannounced, it can only mean trouble!"

They all laughed as Quinn led them through the house and to the shaded back deck. Louisa grabbed a pitcher of ice tea from the refrigerator and four glasses from a cupboard. They sat under the big umbrella as Louisa poured the tea.

Levi looked at his watch. "Now, Louisa, it's just about quitting time, and I'm sure the sheriff wouldn't mind if I had a cold beer."

Quinn laughed as he stood and headed to the kitchen. As soon as he returned and handed Levi his beer, the sheriff looked at Quinn and Louisa and said, "I feel embarrassed to admit we have not made any progress in determining who the man is who has you both in his sights. Because of all the other investigations we are pursuing, nothing much has been accomplished with your important matter."

Quinn looked at him. "Leroy, we totally understand. I have been—sorry, I mean *we* have been—busy on this end. We reached out to the guy who made the expensive knife, and we found out it was shipped to a post-office box in Winston-Salem. A postal inspector is a friend of ours, and he's working on finding out who owns the box and if any video exists of anyone picking anything up from that box. Plus, I think the perp probably hasn't recovered from Louisa's deft use of the wine bottle."

Louisa said, "I only wish I had knocked that idiot out when I hit him!"

They all laughed. The sheriff looked at them and said, "Levi and I met with Pastor Kauffmann, Hope, and Hannah today. They have decided the very best thing to do is to get Hope and Hannah as far from Carroll County as they can."

Louisa said, "And exactly where are they suggesting they go?"

Leroy looked at her. "Belize."

There was silence at the table until Quinn said, "Now, that is interesting. For whatever reason, I believe I read or heard of a Mennonite community being in, I think, the northern part of that country."

Levi said, "You win the bonus round, Quinn. That is where they live. In a place called Blue Creek. Seems as if they are a self-sufficient group up there."

Quinn could tell Louisa was deep in thought. "So, Leroy, all this raises a host of questions. The first of which is transportation: How will they get to Belize? Then we have to ask, who will go with them? Finally, who will know where they are staying?"

The sheriff looked at her. "Great questions, Louisa. I wish I had a deputy to spare who could go, but I don't. Now, I'm not worried about the secrecy aspect. Only the pastor and his wife will know exactly where they will be and who they will be with.

"However, another thought occurred to me as we drove over here. The fact is that another killer is trying real hard to kill both of you, but wouldn't it be more difficult for that idiot to accomplish that if you were, say, separated from each other?"

Quinn raised his hand to object. "You just wait a minute, Leroy Jefferson. I see where you are going with this. You're suggesting Louisa go on vacation to Belize while I become the one and only target for our natural-born killer."

Levi piped in and said, "Hey, if you're all that worried about her well-being there, I'll go along too. I'll be the bodyguard."

Louisa smiled at Levi's suggestion. Before she could make a witty remark, Leroy looked at Levi and said, "Not to worry, Levi. Your assignment hasn't changed. You need to work harder on finding who killed Peggy Neufeld!"

Quinn looked at Leroy. "You really are serious about this, aren't you? So, she leaves me and takes Hope and Hannah off to God only knows where in Belize, and I'm stuck here on my own. But who helps protect me from the maniac trying to kill me?"

Leroy leaned forward in his chair and looked at Quinn. "You seem to have forgotten something. Exactly who was the crack shot who killed the mad priest just before he was about to kill you? That's right—me! So, don't fret about not having protection while she is gone. I can be your guardian angel, McSpain. Heck, I might even ask Laneisha if I can move in with you while Louisa is gone!"

All four erupted in laughter at that suggestion. After Louisa stopped laughing, she looked at Leroy. "As much as I hate the thought of leaving the big fella here, I do see where you are coming from, Leroy. I know I could garner some FBI support in Belize City, if I needed it. Let me sleep on your suggestion and see if this handsome man I live with could bear the pangs of separation if I'm gone for a spell. I should also suggest you lock up Libby in the county jail if I'm away. We all know what she might do!"

Quinn choked on the tea he was drinking. "Leroy, thanks for stopping by and suggesting my love object should leave me in a totally helpless state. I should have known you two might be planning to change our lives when I saw you coming up the driveway. Now, get back to your police work before Levi asks to drink beer in the hot tub!"

Good-byes where exchanged before the sheriff and Levi got in their car and drove down the hill. Levi looked at the sheriff. "Well, what do you think? Will she do it?"

"Levi, I'll give you a month off with pay if she doesn't!"

Back at the house, Quinn went to the wine cellar and took out a bottle of his favorite: Lust, from the Michael David vineyard in Lodi, California. Louisa had already set two tables in front of the hot tub.

Once the wine was poured, Quinn was the first to speak. "I'm already bothered by the thought of you being away for some undefined period. Granted, you are the logical choice to be with them while Leroy works on catching the killers.

"But we are retired, and after all the crap we have been through, haven't we done enough? Granted, some idiot is trying to kill us, for whatever reason, and one less target in the area makes some sense. But—crap! The thought of not having you in my arms each day just sucks!"

Louisa took a sip of wine, left her chair, sat in his lap, and cuddled him. A tear slowly floated down her cheek. She nuzzled up under his chin. "This whole plan sucks. I don't want to be away from you for a minute—much less a day, month, or however damn long all this might take. Yet my rational, analytical side is suggesting to my brain that this might be the best plan for Hope and Hannah. I hate the rational side of my brain. Shouldn't it have shut down when I retired?"

Quinn stirred. Her closeness and warmth, as well as the wine, were having a delightful effect on his libido. Louisa suddenly realized the only trip he was focusing on was the immediate one to the hot tub.

She slowly stood in front of him. The setting sun over the western ridge formed a picturesque backdrop behind her. Quinn started to reach for the buttons on her blouse, but she pushed his hands away and licked her lips.

Quinn reached down and grabbed the seat of his chair. He understood his hands were not needed now. Louisa slowly lifted her wineglass and let droplets of red wine flow down her neck.

Before the wine passed her belly button, she let her jeans drop to the grass. She then leaned over and whispered in Quinn's ear, "Thirsty yet, big fella?"

Quinn picked her up in his arms and placed her on the edge of the hot tub. He traced the rim of her ear with his tongue and said, "Now I know why they named this wine 'Lust'!"

✡ ✡ ✡

Missy was shaken as she ran across the street to her place. The information Brad had shared was crazy. She kept thinking of when Tommie had come home with the severe gash on his head. As she kept trying to put two and two together, the sum kept coming up three.

Yet the very thought that Tommie might have tried to kill someone excited her in a strange way. The notion that someone whom she had made mad, passionate love to had the nerve to kill was stirring some primal desire.

She did not hesitate as she picked up her phone and called Tommie.

He answered on the first ring. "Why did you wait so long to call me?" he asked.

She felt excitement surging in her. "I'll be over before you can hang up!"

Tommie saw her coming toward his door. He pushed a button, and the door opened. She crossed the threshold and saw him standing in the kitchen. Before she walked in, he was pouring two glasses of wine.

She walked right up to him and put her arms around him. "Say you missed me, even if it was only for a little bit!"

Tommie rubbed up against her, and she felt his excitement. She kissed him, her tongue finding its way to his. He pulled back and asked, "Have you been drinking beer?"

She gushed. "Yup. Had a beer across the street while I was waiting for you."

He looked at her, let go, and took a sip of wine. "See anyone interesting at the bar while you were there?"

She slowly sipped her wine. "Just the usual suspects. Except that Brad from the newspaper was there. He filled me in on all the shenanigans that went on while I was at the beach. He told me about the poor Mennonite girl who was killed and… something else."

Tommie noticed an inflection in her voice. He cocked his head. "And what was that?"

Missy cleared her throat and drank some more wine. "I guess someone tried to kill the woman who was involved in the killing of that crazy priest. The one who abducted those poor kids. Do you remember that story? It was all over the news up here when it happened."

Tommie took in a gulp of air and tried to keep his emotions in check. He felt his cheeks redden as he took another sip of wine. "I didn't hear about that one. What happened?"

Missy smiled seductively. "Seems somebody tried to kill her in her hot tub but missed, and she hit him over the head with a wine bottle. From what Brad told me, the police haven't found him yet, and he was never treated at a hospital."

Tommie found it strange that Missy was inching closer to him with a devilish look in her eyes. He immediately understood she had figured out what had happened. He also understood that she didn't seem to give a shit that he might be the killer.

He found her reaction somewhat amusing and concerning at the same time. His immediate instinct was to kill her and to reduce the risk of a loose cannon. He had lived and prospered rather well by living with a complete and unforgiving vow of secrecy.

Missy, however, already knew and seemed not to mind. In that moment, she slid right into his arms and, with her left hand, massaged his scalp. Her right hand slid down into the front of his pants. "Oh, baby, your head seems to be all better! And, oh my, I'm so happy the swelling down here is all back!"

With that, she lowered her left hand and slid his sweat pants down to his ankles. She knelt before him and worked her magic. Tommie closed his eyes and felt his knees weaken. He thought, *There is plenty of time to deal with Missy.*

* * *

Levi put the binoculars down and looked at Jeannie Wishart. They had volunteered to pull a shift watching the Estrada compound. They were sitting on top of a ledge that provided a direct line of sight into the compound.

They had taken over the post at four in the afternoon and had to stay until eleven that night. They had been watching the compound for over an hour and had not seen any activity. Levi looked at her and said, "Are we sure anybody is home?"

Jeannie put the binoculars down. "The report from the last shift was that Estrada and his sidekick, Medina, have been there for the past four days. The only movement they saw was Estrada and Medina going back and forth from the house to the barn."

Levi admired Jeannie's lean figure, which was accentuated by her tight blue jeans and formfitting camouflage top. Her hair was pulled back in a bun and set under her baseball cap.

Jeannie caught Levi staring at her chest. "Levi, seriously, just stop that! Stop thinking they're fake 'cause they're real. It's a family thing. All the women on my mother's side are amply endowed. My genetics, coupled with my daily exercise routine, keep them in shape."

Levi looked somewhat skeptical; he seemed to be deeply considering what she had said.

Jeannie leaned over. "No, Levi, you can't touch them. Get over it!"

Levi blushed and looked at her. "Wow, so there's nothing artificial 'bout them sisters. No, sirree!" he blurted out. He cocked his head back and asked, "Are you dating anyone?"

Jeannie muffled her laugh. "Levi, aren't you still dating that wild girlfriend of yours? What is her name? It's Felicity, isn't it?"

Levi rolled his eyes. "I'm still in the clutches of that wildcat! She still kinda likes me, I guess."

Jeannie grinned. "Didn't she about kill you when you had your affair with Libby? What the hell was that all about? Now, I'm not suggesting you aren't special in your own way, but with all her money, she could probably get just about any man she wanted."

"Yep, any man. Except Quinn McSpain. That is a whole other story, though. Listen, I was her boy toy—pure and simple. I done lost all my common sense with that woman. Should have known better, but I was flying high with her money and power, but it all came crashing down one day. Should have known it would have. I learned a valuable lesson, though. I'll never be that stupid again. Nope. Never! What about you, Wishart? Weren't you married once?"

She looked away. "I was, Levi, but it was a mistake. I made the mistake of not taking a hard look at that man's character. He turned out to be abusive and a slacker to boot. It didn't last a year. I even got it annulled. And that is important because I'm Catholic. My marriage and divorce happened a long time ago, Levi, and I'm much more cautious now when I get into the courtship game. I need to meet the right guy because I want to have a child someday. And the biological clock is ticking away."

Levi looked at her and took her hand. "Jeannie, I believe you would be a wonderful mother. But until that happens… could I get a hug?"

They both muffled their laughter and smiled at each other. Jeannie was first to notice movement in the compound. The main garage door opened, and Medina pulled out and stopped in front of the house.

Medina got out of the driver's side, and Estrada and Elva came out of the house. Estrada got into the driver's side, and Medina climbed into the passenger side. Elva sat in the back seat.

Levi put the binoculars down and reached for his radio. Another one of the sheriff's vehicles was parked several miles away. It was closer to Highway 52. Jeannie and Levi ran toward the all-terrain vehicle, heading down the trail to where it was parked.

Estrada smiled as he drove slowly up to his entry gate. He pushed the button clipped to the car's visor, and the gate opened. He drove over the bridge and took a right on the dirt road. He looked at Medina and said, "You know they are watching us. They have been waiting for us to make a move, so let's see what they do. Get the camera ready to video them if they stop us. I don't think they will, my brother, but you never know."

What Medina didn't know was that, while the Carroll County deputy and DEA agent were following his truck, the DEA surveillance satellite was also tracking their every move. Only a handful of staff at the sheriff's department knew the satellite tracking was on.

Levi disengaged the parking brake after they got into his truck. He hit the gas and tore out of the hidden ditch the truck was parked in. He knew Estrada couldn't be too far ahead.

Wishart called on the radio and found out that Estrada was no more than a quarter mile ahead. Levi backed off the accelerator when they came to the peak of a tall incline on Highway 52. They could see Estrada's truck in the early darkness.

While Estrada and Medina were heading toward Hillsville, it was anyone's guess as to where they might be headed. The mystery didn't last long, though, because when Estrada passed through the intersection of Highways 52 and 58, he took a left into the Food Lion's parking lot.

Levi turned in as well and parked by the Pizza Hut. He looked at Wishart. "*Fuck*!"

* * *

Leroy Jefferson walked into his office just after the crack of dawn. He liked to get in early to clean up all the odds and ends that needed attention. He also knew this day would be hectic and busy. He had set up a meeting with Pastor Kauffmann, Hope, Quinn, and Louisa.

If this trip to Belize was to happen, they needed to set up the logistics quickly, and there were so many questions to be answered. He already knew Quinn was not too happy about the thought of Louisa going to Belize with Hope and Hannah.

As he took a sip of coffee, he realized he had lost track of time. Levi stuck his head into the sheriff's office. "They are all here, boss."

Leroy stood and grabbed his file folder with his free hand as he balanced his coffee cup in the other. He looked around the table. Quinn and Louisa were talking with Jeannie Wishart. Levi sat next to Jeannie. Hannah waved a little wave to each of them.

The sheriff said, "Good morning, y'all. Since the clock is ticking, let's quickly get our plan in place, as far as Belize goes. Pastor, what have you got for us?"

Pastor Kauffmann looked at them all. "I have talked extensively with Pastor John in Blue Creek. All the arrangements have been made on their end to provide safe passage to Blue Creek from Belize City and living accommodations for Hope and Hannah in Blue Creek. A story has been set up to inform any inquiring minds. They'll say Hope and Hannah are the pastor's cousins who are relocating from Canada. Because of her experience, Hope will work in their little restaurant. Hannah will be enrolled in their local school.

"One of the pastor's nephews will work with Louisa while she is there. He is one of the three appointed constables. He works with the Belize police official who covers Blue Creek. While there is very little crime in Blue Creek, these three part-time constables have great insight into the community."

Louisa put her hand up. The pastor stopped talking. She looked at everyone before she said, "Pastor, I'm certain Blue Creek is as peaceful as any place can be in Belize. But times have changed. I did a little research on the area, and it looks as if Blue Creek might not be as bucolic as it once was.

"In August 2015, a Bell Four Oh Five helicopter mysteriously landed in Blue Creek and was abandoned. That's right. A very expensive aircraft was landed and abandoned. The Belize Defence Force investigated and took possession of the helicopter.

"I have checked with my FBI sources in Belize City, and they suggested that, while Blue Creek borders La Union,

Mexico, and Guatemala, those borders are about as porous as any borders can be. However, I was also told that, for all intents and purposes, there is very little crime in Blue Creek and Shipyard, a neighboring village. The modern Evangelical Mennonites live in Blue Creek, while the conservative Kleine Gemeinde Mennonites live in Shipyard."

After Louisa stopped talking, the pastor smiled and said, "Looks as if someone has done her homework. While everything you said is true, Louisa, I must state that, all things considered, Hope and Hannah will be much safer in Blue Creek than in Carroll County."

All eyes turned to Hope as she began to speak. "I must thank all of you for working so hard to keep me and Hannah safe. I believe our lives are in peril if we stay here. I am convinced we must flee to save our lives."

Quinn reached down and squeezed Louisa's hand. She smiled and said, "I agree with Hope, and I am ready to travel and to stay with them for as long as it takes. I suggest we get moving as fast as we can. Also, the fewer people who know of this plan, the better."

Jeannie Wishart said, "I have arranged for a DEA jet to pick them up in Greensboro and fly them directly to Belize City. However, we must decide on how soon you want to make the trip. I will drive them to the airport."

Hope looked at the pastor and said, "Hannah and I can be ready in forty-eight hours."

Louisa looked at Quinn. "So can I," she said.

"This, I believe," said the sheriff, "is the very best we can do to protect you. I promise to use every resource available to catch the killers."

Wishart looked at Hope and said, "I'll pick you both up in two days."

Quinn and Louisa followed Leroy back to his office. Once the door was closed, Leroy asked Louisa, "Are you sure you want to do this?"

"Leroy, I don't want to leave this man, but I just can't say no to that wonderful mother and her daughter. We are doing the right thing. But, Leroy, I need a favor while I'm gone."

"Anything, Louisa. Just ask."

Louisa smiled. "Could you stash Libby Thomas in the county lockup—at least until *I get back*?"

☆ ☆ ☆

Missy was exhausted. Tommie had exploded with a strange sexual rage, which she had countered with one of her own. She sensed that even though they had been together in the same bed, the moment had propelled them to separate erotic solar systems.

She knew she should be frightened of this man, but she also knew there was so much to learn about him. From the very first moment she met him, she knew he kept a million secrets locked up in his mind. She also realized this might be the most dangerous path she would ever follow in her life.

She quietly slipped out of bed and headed to the kitchen. The need for coffee was overpowering her. Tommie opened one eye and watched her walk away from the bed. He looked up at the ceiling. He knew Missy had already crossed the line. She now knew something that could hurt him.

That thought was troubling. He had lived the life he wanted because he could totally control his life. No one was allowed in his life; he had never broken that cardinal rule, but his affection for Missy was clouding his normally clear and cold thinking.

There was no doubt in his mind that she took him to new and amazing sexual realms, but he asked himself whether letting her live was worth the risk. His mind and logic kept saying no. With each minute she lived, she was a risk to his survival.

His train of thought was interrupted when Missy returned to the bedroom with two cups of coffee. He admired her naked torso as she approached. "Is black OK for you?" she asked, and Tommie nodded. "So, what's next, Tommie? You gonna let me into your world, or are you gonna kill me? I'm not stupid. I could have gone to the cops here in Galax and told them about the bump on your head. But I didn't. You are the most exciting man I'll probably ever meet here in the butt end of Virginia. You have probably done more shit than I could ever dream of. But I thought about that last night, and I really don't give a rat's ass about any of that. Sure, you might just look at me as another piece of ass. Well, I'm all of that, and I know you appreciate that. So, my friend with the great pecker, you gotta decide exactly what you want here.

"Maybe you've killed a lot of people. I haven't killed one; I have done some bad shit, but I've never done anything like that. The very thought, however, of blasting some fuck out of this world…well, it sort of excites me. Listen, I know I already have a one-way ticket to hell. Nothing I can do with you will change any of that."

Tommie propped himself up on one elbow. "Don't you have to work today?"

Missy laughed. "I do, and I'm outta here."

She reached down and gave his manhood one more squeeze before she left the bedroom.

Tommie took a sip of coffee and thought about how soon he would punch her one-way ticket *to hell.*

CHAPTER 19

Louisa sat across the aisle from Jeannie Wishart in the Falcon 2000S they were flying in. Hope and Hannah sat on the other side. They were totally transfixed by what they saw outside the window.

"I must say, Jeannie," said Louisa, "looks as if the DEA has a nice budget for jet aircrafts."

Jeannie laughed. "Louisa, this fine flying machine was acquired by us when a certain significant drug dealer in California was finally caught. The DEA is blessed with the ability to acquire many a fine toys from those who so blatantly break our laws."

"We weren't so fortunate to get such great toys during my days with the bureau," said Louisa. "We were lucky to get decent cars to drive around."

Jeannie smiled. "Louisa, I have heard great things about what you accomplished during your days with the FBI. Many female agents might not be where they are today if not for all the glass ceilings you broke."

"Listen, kiddo, I did work hard to get things done in that male-dominated bastion, but it was worth every minute of those long hours I put in. It took a toll, though. I had no personal life. It was all work, work, and more work. I really didn't find happiness until I met Quinn. He has been the love I never had. And, to be honest, our love is a kind I thought I would never have. This interruption will be a test. I haven't been away from him at all.

"I'll worry about him falling prey to the idiot who is trying to kill us. I know he will worry himself sick about me and these two while we are in Belize. I know he will work overtime with the sheriff to get enough evidence on those killers. What's more, he was hurt by Peggy Neufeld's brutal murder. He will probably put himself out there—that is, make himself more visible—to bait the asshole who is trying to kill us."

The less-than-two-hour flight ended quickly as Jeannie and Louisa continued their conversation. The fasten-your-seat-belt sign came on as the plane descended through the clouds, and soon it touched down at the airport.

The pilot taxied to a hangar where several cars were parked. After the copilot had lowered the stairs, Jeannie and Louisa led Hope and Hannah down to the tarmac. Louisa recognized the first person walking in her direction, Special Agent Ben Roberts. She and he had worked together some twenty years ago in New York. She smiled as he approached with his arms extended. "My God, Roberts. What in God's name are you doing here?" Louisa asked.

"I know. You think I should be retired by now. Well, I almost am. I'm assigned to the office in El Salvador, but I work out of the office at the embassy here in Belize. I plan to retire in less than a year, and I plan to stay at a place I bought near the beach. So, my being here works out perfectly for me. But the real question is, what in the hell are you doing on a DEA jet landing here with two Mennonite women? Didn't you retire some years ago, Louisa?"

"I did, Ben, but for some reason, my stars are never in proper alignment, so I always end up helping out folks in crazy situations. I'll fill you in on it all over a beer later."

Ben turned and took the arm of the older man standing close to him. "Louisa, this is Pastor John from Blue Creek."

Louisa put out her right hand and shook hands with the pastor.

"Louisa, we are blessed to have a person of your abilities help us out with this terrible matter. Mister Ben has filled me in on your illustrious career fighting crime with the FBI."

Ben winked at her when the pastor finished.

Pastor John turned and motioned the much taller and younger man to step forward. "Louisa, this is my cousin Badgett. He will stay with you while you are with us, and he'll help with whatever needs to get done."

As Badgett stepped forward, Louisa was taken with his physical presence. He was at least six feet six inches tall and very physically fit. Louisa was doing her best not to stare at his tan and muscled arms.

"My pleasure to meet you, Louisa. I hope I can provide whatever you need during your stay with us here in Blue Creek."

Louisa smiled while the other introductions were made. Badgett went over to a large, white van and pulled it closer to them.

As soon as Hope and Hannah were inside, Jeannie took Louisa's hand and said, "Listen, we have to fly right back to Greensboro. I'm sure Ben Roberts will provide whatever you need while you are here. I wish I could stay to help, but they need me in Carroll County. Listen, if you need anything, though, just let me know because I think I would really like to know that hunky Badgett a little bit better!"

They both laughed as they hugged. Jeannie waved to them all as the stairs were retracted back into the plane. Louisa walked back to van, where Ben was standing.

He was holding a large, black case, which looked big enough to hold a tuba. He undid the snaps and opened the top. Louisa immediately felt safer when she looked at the assortment of weapons inside.

"Listen, Hawke," he said, "I hope you never have to use any of these. However, these will help if danger comes to your doorstep. Use this satellite phone if you need to reach me. I have a helicopter at my disposal too. I can also call upon the resources of the Belize Defence Force if shit hits the proverbial fan. I'm not going to follow you in my car, though; doing so might call attention to your presence. You will be in good hands with Badgett and the Mennonite resources in Blue Creek."

Louisa smiled at Roberts and gave him a big hug. "Thanks, my friend, and don't worry. I'll call if I need you."

After she sat in her seat, Badgett pulled the van around to a private gate and said something to a guard, who swung the gate open. Within ten minutes, they were heading north on the Old Northern Highway. Traffic was very light away from the airport.

Louisa was sitting next to Pastor John. "How long is this drive, Pastor?" she asked.

He looked at his watch. "It will take an hour to get to Orange Walk Town on this road. After that, we will leave this beautiful pavement and navigate the dirt road for about two hours."

Hope's and Hannah's eyes were glued to the windows. They were looking at the countryside passing by. They had a good look at it since Badgett had to drive slowly in order to negotiate the large, deep potholes that dotted the narrow dirt road.

The scenery along the way was beautiful. People were walking along the dirt road and waving at them. Trucks carrying loads of sugarcane passed by. The land seemed alive with fields overflowing with nature's bounty.

The pastor looked at both of them. "As you see, Hope, this is a very poor country. There aren't three hundred fifty thousand people who call Belize home. Most people in this part of the country are dirt poor. Most locals who hope to make more money live in or near the tourist attractions or the resort areas. Where we are going isn't near any of that. We are the farmers who practically feed the whole country.

"We have cows with big horns. They are suited for the heat. Our Mennonite community has thousands upon thousands of acres, which we farm. We also grow rice and have a rice factory to process it; we sell it in Belize and Mexico."

The pastor continued to tell Hope and Hannah about the country and the many roles the Mennonites played in Belize. Louisa looked at the road ahead and thought she caught Badgett looking at her in the rearview mirror.

Badgett slowed to turn at San Felipe, a small village. Pastor John looked at Louisa. "We will be in Blue Creek soon," he said.

"None too soon, Pastor, because this road has played havoc with my old back!" Louisa said.

The pastor laughed, as did Badgett, who was slowly picking up speed. Within ten minutes, Louisa looked straight ahead but couldn't believe her eyes. A large sign ahead, on the right side of the road, read Welcome to Blue Creek.

The road quickly changed from dirt to a wide paved road, with beautiful flowers and trees on both sides. The road curved, turning uphill for at least a mile. The pastor smiled at Louisa and asked, "How is your back now?"

Louisa smiled and gave him a thumbs-up. Badgett slowed near the top of the hill and turned left onto a long driveway. As they drove closer, she saw beautiful horses in the pasture and what looked like thatched guesthouses. At the end of the driveway, Badgett stopped and parked at a large building, which looked like a lodge.

It was perched high on the hilltop, offering a magnificent view. Badgett came around and opened both van doors. Louisa took Badgett's hand as she stepped out. The pastor followed with Hope and Hannah in tow.

Louisa took several steps forward and took in the view. As she did, the front door of the lodge opened, and a woman stepped out. She smiled at Louisa and said, "Hello, my name is Judy. You must be Louisa." She took one of Louisa's hands. "Welcome to Blue Creek. Thank you for bringing Hope and Hannah to us." She then turned to Hannah and said, "Oh my, what a beautiful child!"

Judy picked her up and gave her a warm hug. Hope felt tears welling in her eyes. She looked at Pastor John. "I already feel safer in this glorious place."

He took her over to Judy and said, "This is my wonderful wife, who will do her best to care for you and Hannah."

Judy looked at Badgett and said, "Please take Louisa up to her cabin and get her unpacked. We will be having dinner in about two hours."

"I can do that," he replied, opening a van door for Louisa, who reentered the vehicle.

He turned the van around and drove up a paved road that was steep, winding, and narrow to the very top of the plateau. He stopped in front of a small cottage. It was not far from the edge of the cliff.

Louisa stepped out and took in the view. "This is very nice," she said.

Badgett smiled as he stood beside her. "Yes, it is, and the best part is that it is cooler up here than on the valley floor. The evening breezes will try to convince you that you need a light sweater."

He then went back to the van and took her bags into the cottage. The front of the cottage offered a beautiful view of the entire valley below. The side room was the eat-in kitchen area. The large back bedroom had a bathroom attached.

Badgett put her suitcases on the bed and the heavy bag Jeannie had given her on the couch. He looked at Louisa after he opened the bag. "Do you know how to use all these toys?"

She stood beside him and asked, "The better question is, do you?"

He laughed. "During my years in a unit of the Canadian Special Operations Forces Command, I used most of these at one time or another. But I think you probably used some during your time with the FBI. Unless you were a pencil pusher."

Louisa zipped the bag shut. "Well, I hope that while I'm a guest in Blue Creek, I can teach you a thing or two about these weapons. I understand that only the Mounties can shoot straight up on the frozen Canadian tundra."

Badgett laughed. "Well, look at what we have here—a Yankee with a delightful sense of humor. We shall see about all that in due time, I'm sure."

With that, he headed to the front door. "My cabin is two down from yours. I'm going to shower and change clothes.

I'll come by in an hour; then we'll walk down the hill to the lodge for dinner."

Louisa then started to unpack in anticipation of a shower. She suddenly felt tired from the day's journey but knew that a long, hot shower would feel good. She found the framed picture she had packed of Quinn, which she placed on the table beside her bed.

They had agreed to limit their calls to Sundays and just one a week. They understood the need to limit the possibility of any communication being hacked in any way. It didn't take long for her to undress and walk into the shower.

The steaming hot water was the elixir she needed. Her thoughts drifted back to Quinn as her hands washed every part of her body. She knew it might be a long time before they showered together again.

She quickly toweled off when her stomach began to send messages of hunger to her brain. After getting dressed, she stepped outside and could not resist going to the large, white glider to the left of her cabin.

She sat on the side that offered the best view of the valley below. The cool evening breeze flowed through her long red hair. She was intoxicated by the moment, and then someone behind her stopped the glider.

"OK, Louisa Hawke, I hope you are as hungry as I am. Let's get moving down the hill to Judy's kitchen."

Louisa jumped off the glider and looked at Badgett. He was wearing a T-shirt with Bermuda shorts and hiking boots.

Louisa looked at the running shoes she was wearing. "Do you like to run, Badgett?" she asked.

"Well, I do—"

Before he could finish, Louisa started off at full speed down the hill. Badgett took off after her and yelled, "*Oh no you don't, lady*!"

☆ ☆ ☆

Missy hurried from Tommie's house because she knew she would be late for work. She quickly went to her apartment to change. After her shower, she dressed quickly, but before leaving, she sat down at her desk and took out a piece of white stationery.

She sat for a moment and carefully crafted several paragraphs. After finishing, she folded the paper and placed it into an envelope. She wrote an address on it and put a stamp on the corner. She thought for a moment before running out the door of her apartment.

On the sidewalk, she ran to the mailbox on the street corner, next to the hardware store. She smiled as she dropped the letter inside. She crossed the street to the hardware store and thought, *If you kill me, Tommie Cruz, you're fucked*!

☆ ☆ ☆

Quinn felt startled when he awoke. He hadn't been sleeping well since Louisa left for Belize. Her absence was already causing his psyche to ache; he had realized his life was really their life together. He was feeling torn and lonesome without her by his side.

He also missed her cooking. While he found solace in running and biking on the parkway, such physical activity made him hungry. So, he often found himself having lunch at the deli in Fancy Gap and stopping in at the Hardware Bar and Grill in Hillsville.

While such places provided the nourishment he needed, they also exposed him to unwanted attention. No more than a week after Louisa left, he was enjoying a wonderful chicken salad at the deli. He was reading the *New York Times* on his iPad, but he looked up and saw Libby come through the front door.

He heard a hoot from the kitchen and knew his friend Sharon had seen Libby as well. Oh well, he thought. Had to happen sooner or later. He set his iPad down and took a sip of his ice tea.

Libby's smile was as broad as Fancy Gap's mountain range. She was wearing a very expensive halter top and designer shorts. Within a moment, she was standing in front of Quinn. "Well, McSpain, this must be my lucky day. OK, I'll fess up. I only stopped because I saw that big, black Dodge Ram of yours in the parking lot. But I am kinda hungry, and I know you won't mind if I sit with you."

Quinn motioned for her to sit in the chair on the other side of the table. Instead, she pulled the chair next to him closer, sat down, and said, "So, my dearest love object, I need to set a few things straight."

Just as she finished, Sharon came around the corner and stopped at Quinn's table. "Now, Libby, I just heard what you said. So, we need to set a few things straight. The very first is that Quinn is *my* love object, and that means he is taken."

Libby put her hand up in protest. "Girl, you need to back up into the kitchen and mind your own business—or I might buy this darn deli just to fire you! Get back there, and bring me a tuna salad and some tea. Get!"

Quinn was biting his tongue as Sharon slowly walked away with an extra wiggle in her backside. Libby huffed and said, "I swear. That woman just likes to piss me off when you're around. And especially when your Louisa isn't with you. Now, speaking of Louisa, my confidential sources tell me your girlfriend is nowhere to be found. All the Quinn sightings have been of you in a solitary state. Pray tell, my friend, what do I need to know? Kick that redhead to the curb, did you?" She pulled back her blond hair and batted her eyelashes at him.

"Libby, Libby, Libby! Why so much concern about my and Louisa's whereabouts? With all your important business deals occurring throughout the country, I'm surprised you have any time at all for what's happening in tiny Carroll County."

She laughed. "You know damn well I can buy anything I want. Sure, I've had some interesting opportunities lately with some interesting men who have crossed my path, but they are all fucking boring. I know exactly what I want here at home, but someone just isn't cooperating. So, tell me the truth. Where is Louisa?"

Quinn stared at her. "Libby, this is none of your business. But I know how persistent you can be, so I'll tell you on one condition: you won't tell a soul. Let's make another condition: you won't sneak into my place for no good reason. Can you live with that?"

Libby offered a coy smile and nodded in the affirmative.

"OK," said Quinn, "she is in California with her sister who is very sick. Unless some miraculous recovery happens, her sister has less than a few months to live. Louisa neglected her sister when she spent all those years with the FBI. So, now she feels the need to be close to her sister while her sister is still alive. I don't have a clue how long Louisa will be there. Now, that is what's happening, and that is just between you and me."

Libby thought about what Quinn told her. "Well, OK. I guess I can only hope her poor sister hangs on as long as she can. Please pass along to Louisa that I will do my best to make sure you're well attended to on this end."

Just before Quinn could respond, Sharon came around the corner with Libby's lunch. She set the salad and tea down in front of her without saying a word. She offered Quinn a big smile as she left.

Louisa picked up the salad plate and examined it closely. "I bet that bitch thought about spitting in my salad."

Quinn laughed as Libby began eating. They talked for another ten minutes before Libby wiped her mouth with her napkin. “Time to go,” she said. “My dear Artimus has information on a newly born filly that has come from some pretty impressive bloodlines. I know what you’re thinking, McSpain. I am still in the hunt for that perfect horse. The world has heard from me once, and I will do my best to ensure they hear from me again!” She leaned over and gave Quinn a peck on the cheek; she then stood, walked to the door, and left.

Sharon watched her leave before walking to Quinn’s table. “That woman never even pays her bill when she is here!”

Quinn laughed. “Not a problem. Add it to mine. I keep tabs on what she owes me.”

Sharon looked at him as he stood. “Now, Quinn, I know your girlfriend hasn’t been with you for a bit, so if you need some help in your kitchen anytime soon, I’d love to help.”

Quinn smiled as he hugged her. “You know, I just might take you up on that!” he said, heading out the door.

Sharon laughed as she watched him get into his truck. *If only, she thought.*

☆ ☆ ☆

More than ten days had passed, and Medina was getting antsy. While all their usual drug deals were going off without a hitch, he believed it was time to resume their search for the woman and little girl who could identify them.

Medina went into Estrada's office in the barn and sat down. Estrada could tell something was bothering Medina, so he asked, "OK, my friend, what's on your mind? Out with it!"

"Jefe, I believe it's time to start looking for that woman again. The cops must be getting tired of watching us. What do you think?"

Estrada smiled. "Oh, my friend, I believe we are on the same page of sheet music, but I am very pleased we waited. You now that little secret bird who works in the sheriff's department—the one who owes us? Well, I got an encrypted message from her. Seems the woman and her daughter have left the area."

"Shit, Duke, did she tell you where they went?"

"No, she didn't, but she suggested we have a little conversation with the pastor at the Mennonite Church because he has been spending time at the sheriff's department. And that makes sense to me. If the woman and her daughter needed help, the pastor would be the person she would go to."

"OK, when do we pay the church a visit?"

Estrada looked out the window of his office and said, "We don't have to, Roger. I sent a message to a computer guru and asked him to look into it. Quickly. It didn't take him long. Seems the pastor has been making many calls to some Mennonite people in Belize. The guru told me there is a Mennonite community in the northern part of that country, very close to the border with Mexico. I'm convinced that is where they went to hide; it is a good place to hide them—but not such a good place any longer *because now we know*!"

☆ ☆ ☆

Missy got a text message from Tommie just before it was time to leave work. She smiled before responding with a thumbs-up. The notion of Tommie cooking dinner for them both was very appealing. She knew he was an accomplished cook and loved to whip up exotic meals.

Within a moment, she was headed out the door. She waved to Karen as she left. She just missed being hit by a pickup truck when she ran across the street, and she yelled at the driver, "Watch where the fuck you're going, you asshole!"

The driver flipped her the bird.

She laughed all the way up the stairs to her apartment. She was torn about what clothes she wanted to wear, though she understood that whatever she wore, she wouldn't wear it for long.

She was dressed and heading to Tommie's in a quick fifteen minutes. When she got to his door, Tommie looked at his camera screen and got to see what she was wearing. He hit the button and watched her enter through the door.

"Well, aren't you the sexy little vixen?" he said, admiring her small denim shorts and the matching denim halter top. He also thought the red stiletto heels were a nice touch.

"So, what have you been up to while I was slaving away at work today? Probably didn't think about me one bit, did you?"

She wrapped her arms around his waist as he opened a bottle of chilled Chardonnay. He filled two glasses and handed one to Missy. She seductively ran her tongue over the edge of the glass and smiled at him.

"Now, Missy, if you aren't hungry right at this moment, we can fuck each other silly for a while."

Missy backed off and looked in the kitchen. "What has my chef whipped up for us tonight? Oh my, is that lobster you're going to cook for us?"

Tommie walked over to the counter and held one of them up. "I'll start cooking these rascals so we can eat. I want you well nourished for the night ahead."

Later, they sat and ate, the wine flowing freely throughout the meal. When they finished, Missy took one of the two tall candles Tommie had lit and placed on the table, and she slowly headed toward his bedroom. He followed her.

Missy set the candle down on the dresser and slowly danced in the candle's shadow. She moved in Tommie's direction, took his hand, and led him to the bed. She slipped his shirt off and licked his nipples with her tongue.

His arousal was immediate. He dropped his shorts to the floor and slid his hands under her halter top, which he flung to the side of the bed. She wiggled out of her shorts as his hands slipped under her buttocks. He picked her up and forced her up against the wall.

They were soon in a rhythmic motion, which began slowly and quickly accelerated, and Tommie turned and took her to the bed. He felt the wetness of her orgasms as she rocked from side to side.

"Is that all you got!" she screamed with pleasure. "I want more!"

Tommie smiled a wicked smile. He wrapped his right hand around her throat and began to squeeze. In a moment, the lack of oxygen to Missy's brain took effect. She exploded, experiencing the most powerful orgasm she had ever felt.

Suddenly her eyes opened, and she looked at Tommie. "Enough!" she choked.

In the next moment, her eyes grew wide in horror when Tommie increased his grip around her neck. He bent down to her left ear and whispered, "I hope you enjoyed *your last supper*!"

CHAPTER 20

As time passed, Hope and Hannah had fallen into their new routines. Hannah had been enrolled at the Linda Vista School and had quickly made new friends. Hope worked at the small restaurant that Pastor John and Judy maintained at the entrance to their property.

Hope enjoyed meeting all the new people in the community who knew she was working there. The story disseminated throughout the community was that Hope and Hannah had moved to Blue Creek from Canada.

No one questioned their past; as with most newcomers to the Blue Creek community, new arrivals were looking to start fresh in a new place and to put the past behind them, so the community respected such wishes. Several young, single men came by the restaurant because they had heard Hope was a widow.

Louisa faced a different kind of adjustment. She started her mornings with long runs or tried to take bicycle rides using Judy's old Schwinn three-speed, which was a challenge due to the hilly terrain.

She would check in with Hope from time to time and would visit the rice factory, where Badgett was the supervisor of the first shift. She was amazed by the fact the factory was a co-op owned by all the Blue Creek residents who could invest.

She found the amount of cooperation among all the members amazing. While there was a wealth of diverse personalities, people didn't seem to put themselves ahead of others for personal gain.

Louisa was sitting in front of the lodge and admiring the amazing collection of exotic birds, which Pastor John had assembled in a large, screened-in area. She saw John walking up the path to the lodge with another man.

They stopped when they reached her. "Louisa," said the pastor, "I'd like you to meet my friend Wallace. He lived in Virginia some time ago and would like to talk with you. I will leave you two to visit."

Louisa looked at the handsome man standing in front of her. He had a full head of silver hair and a warm smile. He took her hand. "Louisa, good to meet you," he said. "I understand you have come to us from Virginia. May I ask from which part?"

Louisa smiled. "Well, Wallace, I live in Fancy Gap, and I bet you have never heard of it, have you?"

Wallace looked at her. "Well, is the Lakeview Restaurant still open? And how about the Labor Day Flea Market in Hillsville?"

Louisa hesitated for a moment. "Wow, you know a little about Fancy Gap! Did you live there?"

He turned and looked at the birds. "I remember a little about that area, but I was hurt in a plane crash many years ago and was in critical condition for a long time. Pastor John and his friends found me and cared for me. I've been here ever since. I love these wonderful people; they have been very good to me. This is my home."

She was about to ask him another question when Badgett drove up on his motorcycle. She had made arrangements with Badgett to have lunch with him at the small restaurant not far from the mill.

She stood and smiled at Wallace. "So nice to meet you, Wallace. Let's visit again soon. I can tell you more about Fancy Gap."

He stood and shook her hand. "I'd like that."

Louisa got behind Badgett on the motorcycle. "So, does Wallace have a last name?" she asked.

She barely heard him as they drove off. "I think it's Thrasher," he said.

Inside the restaurant, he held a chair for her as she sat down. He was wearing a white dress shirt with the sleeves cut off under bib overalls cut into shorts. He took off his straw hat and wiped the sweat off his brow with his bandana.

"Looks as if someone earned his keep at the mill today," Louisa said.

"Louisa, what I think I really should do is get you a job at the mill. We have a nice opening in the warehouse; you would help load and unload trucks. I bet you don't know how to operate a forklift."

"Au contraire, my friend. I did learn how to do that many years ago, when I was working in an undercover operation. I'm sorry to inform you that I simply can't do that anymore, though. After all, young man, I am retired."

Badgett laughed. "You're too young to be retired!"

Louisa laughed. "You're at least fifteen years younger than I am. You're a baby."

The waitress stood there for a moment as they talked. She looked at Badgett, whom she knew, and she said, "So, are you going to talk with your younger sister all day, or do you plan on having lunch?"

Louisa gave her a high five as Badgett bent over in laughter. Once the waitress had their orders, she winked at Louisa and left. Louisa looked at him and said, "Now, that is a very perceptive person! But, no, I can't go to work in the factory. I need my beauty naps in the afternoon."

When their lunch was brought to the table, Louisa looked at him. "I went for a run down the mountain this morning. After several turns, I happened upon an airfield. What is that all about?"

"I'm surprised you didn't see it while you were up on the ridge. I think you can see it from the glider. Well, that is our own little airstrip. We have several crop dusters and four smaller planes, which we use for different reasons. The oldest plane is a vintage Piper J-Three, which is in great shape.

"Sometimes we need to get someone to the hospital in Belize City in a hurry, and the planes are very useful in such emergencies. All the planes and equipment are owned by the co-op. Seven of us are licensed pilots. Do you fly?"

"I did a long time ago. I haven't taken the controls in years."

"So, we have an opportunity here. We must take one of the crop dusters up. We can fly over Guatemala and Mexico, as well as the Mayan ruins. They are beautiful from the air." Badgett then looked at his watch. "But I'm having too much fun here. Time to get back to work. You should stay and finish your lunch, and while you're at it, please pick up the bill."

"Right. Get out of here. I'll walk back."

He stood, put his straw hat back on, and waved to people on the way out. The waitress came by with the check. "How well do you know Badgett?" she asked.

Louisa frowned and looked at her. "Well, not very well. Why do you ask?"

The waitress leaned over and looked into her eyes. "Many of us have tried to—well, let's see—make ourselves available to the man. But no one has succeeded. But I watched the way he looked at you, and he thinks you're someone special!"

Louisa blushed.

☆ ☆ ☆

Quinn had finally set up a meeting with Bruce Sprinkle, the postal inspector. He drove down to Winston-Salem to meet him at the post office on Healy Drive. He hadn't seen Bruce since the man had helped him on a kickback case, and that was some fifteen years ago.

Sprinkle came into the lobby to meet Quinn. "Well, McSpain, you ole rascal. I'd like to suggest that time has treated you well, but I must be honest. You look like shit!"

Quinn held out his hand. "So, I'd be lying if I told you that you looked that good!"

They both laughed as Sprinkle led him back to an office. When they sat down, Bruce said, "If my intel is right, aren't you shacked up with that great-looking redhead who was some bigwig in the FBI?"

"Well, my friend, I am enjoying the company of a truly beautiful woman, and she makes me very happy. I only hope your intel about the prick who had that knife shipped here is helpful."

"This is your lucky day, McSpain. We checked out the name of the person who rented the post-office box. You guessed it: the name was an alias. However, what he didn't know is that our hidden camera snapped a picture of him when he purchased the box. It's not much as far as pictures go, but it is something for you to chew on. I think he might have known the pic was taken. I ran it through some facial-recognition programs but didn't get a hit."

Quinn looked at the eight-by-ten print. "You're right, Bruce. This isn't much. He was smart enough to keep moving, and his doing so affected the quality. Who knows? Maybe someone in my neck of the woods will recognize something in this picture."

Bruce stood, shook Quinn's hand, and said, "Godspeed, my friend, and I hope you catch that *son of a bitch*!"

* * *

Estrada was pleased with the progress he and Medina had made since evading detection when they left his compound in Hillsville. They had taken a flight from Raleigh, which took them to Cancún. The fake passports and driver's licenses had worked perfectly.

The arrangements he made with one of El Chapo's lieutenants would serve him well. They were met at the Cancún airport by Joel "Big Daddy" Suarez and Mario "Peanut" Larios. Estrada knew them both because together they had coordinated several drug shipments from the Mexican border to Hillsville.

He also knew that both were accomplished killers and would be valuable when they eventually crossed the border from Mexico to Blue Creek. The four met for dinner on the evening of Estrada's arrival.

They decided on the La Habichuela restaurant, where Suarez had reserved a small private room. They all met at the front entrance at seven o'clock. They were met by the maître d', who hugged all four men. As he led them to the room, many staff members paused because they understood exactly who had entered the restaurant.

After the group was seated and served a round of drinks, Suarez said, "Hey, my good friend Duke! So, good to be with you again! But I'm a little surprised. You let a woman and a little girl slip through your hands. Man, the Duke Estrada I once knew would have quickly arranged for a funeral for such easy prey!"

Estrada blushed for a moment, taking a sip of beer to buy himself a moment. Medina muffled a laugh as he looked at Estrada. "Sorry, boss. I wasn't laughing at you. They just don't understand how crazy all this shit has been. There was even a fucking possessed witch who killed Solis!"

"I heard about this woman," Suarez replied. "Now, that is some scary shit I wouldn't fuck with."

Larios shook his head. "We will not be going into a den of bunny rabbits when we cross the border into Blue Creek. I have a cousin who lives in La Union on our side, but his wife works for the Mennonites in Blue Creek. She works in a small kitchen for one of their leaders. She knows what is going on there and will be valuable to us. Now, Duke, we cannot underestimate these people. They all hunt and are very strong.

"They pride themselves on taking care of their own. Trust me, I would expect them to be prepared for a visit. But we will have the element of surprise when we visit. When in La Union, we will stay with my cousin for a couple of days. She will fill us in on what is happening there."

Suarez looked at them all. "Let us celebrate our reunion tonight and dance with the pretty women in Cancún. We have a long drive ahead of us tomorrow. Salud, *my brothers*!"

☆ ☆ ☆

Tommie finished cleaning up from his delightful lobster dinner and went to his bedroom to change clothes. He knew it would be best to dispose of Missy's body before the sun came up. After he changed into work clothes, he wrapped her body in a sheet and carefully stuffed it into a black body bag.

Within ten minutes, he had the bag neatly placed in the back of his truck's bed and under the bed cover. He drove out of Galax and headed west on Highway 58. It was now two o'clock in the morning, and as he expected, there was no one else on the road.

It took a good forty-five minutes for him to reach his destination. He pulled off the road about a half mile from the Lover's Leap Overlook. He had hiked in that area before and knew of a trail that led down the mountain to a small cave.

In no time, he had the body bag slung over his shoulder and was carefully following the trail down the mountain. He used his flashlight to search for the small entry to the cave. He stopped when he noticed a small indentation to his right—the entrance.

It didn't take long for him to drag the body bag into the cave. He hunched over and placed it as far back as he could. Once he was satisfied with where it was, he stopped for a moment and looked back at the bag.

He muttered a few words. "*It was fun while it lasted, bitch*!"

✲ ✲ ✲

Louisa looked at her satellite phone. It had been some time since she had spoken to Quinn. She understood why it was prudent to limit any form of communication, but she was already looking forward to their call in two days. She also missed sharing some great wines with him.

She walked out to the glider, hoping to catch a summer-night breeze because the day was hotter and more humid than usual. She found little relief. The breeze had taken the night off.

She pushed the glider faster, trying to create a cooling effect. She was startled when she felt someone behind her pushing the glider faster. "Now, is that better?" Badgett asked.

He slowed the glider, jumped on, and sat across from her. His muscular physique was emphasized by the tight tank top he was wearing.

"So, tell me," she said, "when can we expect some cooler weather? On days like today, I wish for an air-conditioned cabin."

Badgett laughed. "Louisa, it will be a few months before the late-fall winds blow in. Until then, we sweat. However, there is a source of relief I don't think you know about."

Louisa cocked her head. "Well, Badgett, don't hold back. Spill the beans. Please!"

He looked at her. "Well, Pastor John owns a lovely place on a beautiful freshwater lake. He has some thirty or so acres. All his children have their own cabins, and he was kind enough to give one to me as well. The water is crystal clear and cool. A dock extends out into the water, which we swim off. It is a beautiful place. I'm surprised John hasn't told you about it."

Louisa grinned. "I'm surprised you haven't told me about it sooner! Exactly how far from here is it?"

"Well, if we take my motorcycle, we can be there in fifteen minutes."

Louisa put her right foot out and slowly brought the glider to a stop. She jumped out. "So, what are we waiting for? Do I need a bathing suit?"

Badgett laughed. "You won't need one."

Within five minutes, they were dodging potholes, with Louisa holding on to him for dear life. Her fingers felt every ripple of his ripped abs. Her knees squeezed the seat for support. She felt an adrenaline rush as he sped up on the curves.

Soon after a tight curve, Louisa looked up to see a lake looming in the distance. Badgett brought the motorcycle to a stop in front of a large cabin. They both were silent as they regarded the beautiful, expansive water.

Badgett turned to look at her. "You can let go now."

Louisa blushed a bit. She threw her leg over the motorcycle. "This is truly beautiful."

Badgett pulled two cabin chairs together and sat in one. Louisa sat in the other. A gentle breeze was coming off the lake. "If only we had something to drink," Louisa whispered.

"Your wish might have just come true. Sit tight."

Louisa watched him stand and go inside his cabin. She relaxed even more, letting herself slump in the chair. The screen door opened, and Badgett came out holding a bottle and two glasses. He set them down on the small table in front of them. The glasses had ice cubes in them.

"OK," Louisa said. "What poison have you picked to kill me with?"

"Well, Louisa, I promise this will not kill you. It is German moonshine. This is a Mennonite recipe that has been passed on for generations. No, it won't kill you, but you will forget about the heat," he said, laughing.

Louisa leaned forward and picked up a glass. She filled it to the top, put it to her lips, and took a small sip. "Nice…this is very nice. I taste the alcohol, but it isn't overwhelming. It has a bit of a fruity taste to it. I like it."

"I thought you would," he said, and he filled his glass.

She looked at him. "So, why the hell has it taken you so long to tell me about this? I could have been enjoying this two weeks ago!"

She poured herself another glass. A smile was on her face.

Badgett laughed. "Well, I could have, but I wasn't sure you could handle it. After all, I didn't want you acting silly in front of Pastor John and Judy, much less Hope and Hannah."

Louisa took another long sip. "So, are you happy here, Badgett? Don't you ever yearn for all the things you enjoyed in Canada?"

"Louisa, I thought I enjoyed things in my past life, but that's all they were—nothing more than useless things. Here, I have discovered a real life. Yes, it is simple, but that is what I love. I don't miss any part of my former life. Not a thing!" Louisa was about to say something when Badgett stood. "Didn't we come here to cool off? Time to swim, isn't it?"

He laughed as he walked to the dock. Louisa watched him stand on it, slowly take off all his clothes, and jump into the lake.

She felt a sense of excitement she hadn't felt for a while. She looked at her half-filled glass and finished it off. As she stood, she realized her legs were a bit shaky as she walked to the dock.

At the end of the dock, she looked at Badgett, who was waist deep in the water. She turned away slightly as she began to undress. Then she smiled and turned toward him as she took off her top and wiggled out of her shorts.

She took two steps and dived into the water. She sensed the immediate relief of the cool water on her body. The sensation was euphoric as she swam circles around Badgett.

"So, you think you are a good swimmer, lady?" he said, and he pointed to a floating raft some twenty feet out in the lake.

He dived under the surface and started swimming to the raft. Louisa wasted no time; she soon caught up to him. Within minutes, she was the first to reach the raft. She laughed when his hand took hold of the end of the raft.

He caught his breath and splashed water in her face. "It's a round trip, lady. Bye-bye!" he yelled, and he pushed off the raft.

Louisa took in a lungful of air and gave chase. She soon realized he was a much stronger swimmer than she had thought.

His hand touched the end of the dock first. He used his other hand to pull himself onto the dock, where he then sat. His feet were dangling in the water when she got to the dock. "Must have taken a wrong turn, didn't you?"

He snickered, and then he offered a hand, which she took. He helped her onto the dock. She sat for a moment before she lay down on her back and looked at the sky. The physical exertion and the moonshine were suddenly colliding.

She laughed as she reached up and ran her hand down his back. "A girl could get used to all this," she whispered.

Badgett slowly turned and looked at her. The setting sun glistened off the water droplets on her naked torso. He slowly bent down and gently kissed her lips. She moaned deeply as she returned his kiss passionately.

Louisa was suddenly lost in the intense ecstasy *of the moment.*

CHAPTER 21

Estrada was tired after the long drive from Cancún. He was less than impressed with what he was now seeing of La Union, Mexico. He looked at Joel Suarez as they pulled into the driveway of what looked like the nicest house in this tiny community.

"Jesus, Joel, this looks like the end of the line, as they say. What the fuck do people do who live here?" Estrada asked.

"Well, my brother, I really don't know, but I'm certain Mario's cousin will fill us in."

Just then, the front door opened, and a man walked toward their SUV as they got out. Larios looked at the man. "Hey, my cousin, how the fuck are you? Wish I could say I missed visiting you here, but that would be a lie."

They all laughed as introductions were made, and they headed into the house. Eric Torres was the local pharmacist, and he sometimes worked with the cartel to move drugs across the border. He was probably the wealthiest man in town.

His wife, Tanya, had prepared some food and drinks for them. Medina was pleased because he was famished from the long trip. As they ate and drank, Estrada looked at Torres.

"Tell me, my friend, what do we have to look forward to when we cross that river and go to that place?"

Eric Torres looked at the four men. "Do not take this task lightly, my friends. These are serious, hardworking people, and they are not afraid to defend what is theirs. Nothing is easy for the Mennonites. Nothing is given to them. I have great respect for how they stick together and share among themselves. I think it is wise that you are few in numbers. You must go in quickly, kill your prey, and get out. While they are peaceful people, they all have weapons and know how to use them."

Tanya Torres listened to her husband talk. She understood they must work with the cartel and the likes of Joel Suarez, but she was not happy about it. She and many other men and women from La Union crossed the river each day to work for the Mennonites. They paid very good wages and were kind people.

However, she was torn about what was about to go down and unsure of what she should or might do. She stopped thinking about it when Eric looked at her. "Hey, my sweetest wife, we need some more beer and food. The men are still hungry!"

She smiled as she went to the kitchen.

Suarez looked at Torres. "So, when do you suggest we cross the river and take care of business?"

Torres looked at him. "Amigo, today is Sunday. I suggest you wait until Tuesday to set your plan in motion. Tanya will cross the river on Monday morning and go to work as usual. She will know exactly where the mother and little girl are and make sure they are still in the cabins they have been staying in. She will fill us in when she gets back here on Monday afternoon."

Suarez looked at them all. "So, Tuesday it is. We will get all our weapons ready on Monday."

They all nodded in agreement. Tanya heard every word they said, and suddenly she knew what *she had to do.*

☆ ☆ ☆

Claire Kelly shook off the sand from her flip-flops when she stopped at her mailbox. It was on the path from the beach in Rodanthe. The weather that day at the Outer Banks was perfect. She hated to leave the sand and surf, but her boyfriend, Rolando, was due back at their beach house at five o'clock.

She looked inside the mailbox and removed several letters. Some she recognized as bills, but one stuck out and caught her attention. It had a return address from her girlfriend Missy, who had recently spent some time with her.

She smiled as she walked up the front stairs to the beach house. She noticed that Rolando's Porsche was already in the driveway. He greeted her with a kiss as she entered the kitchen. "Looks as if someone had a great day at the beach," he said.

Claire smiled as she took the letter opener out of the kitchen drawer.

"Who is that from, sweetie? One of your other boyfriends?" he asked.

She took out the letter from the envelope and began to read the note. She sat down at the kitchen table and let out a gasp. Rolando looked at her. "What's wrong, baby?"

Claire pushed the letter toward him. He picked it up and began reading. "Oh shit," he exclaimed.

Claire took it from him and read it aloud.

> Claire,
> When you get this letter, please call me to make sure I'm all right. If you can't contact me in any way, shape, or form, please check with Karen Boyd at the hardware store to see if she knows where I'm at. If she doesn't, call Sheriff Leroy Jefferson in Carroll County, Virginia, and tell him that Tommie Cruz, who lives in Galax, was the one who tried to kill the FBI woman. He is also the person who, if you can't find me, killed me. I love you!
> Missy

They both looked at each other in shock. Rolando said, "What are you going to do?"

Claire started to sob. "I'm going to call Karen and then the sheriff. This is so fucking scary. Hand me my cell phone. I will try calling her."

She punched in Missy's cell number into her phone. It rang for a few moments until she heard, "This number is no longer in use."

She dropped her phone and cried *harder.*

☆ ☆ ☆

Quinn looked forward to his second cup of coffee that morning. He was concerned about Louisa missing their scheduled call last night. He knew that if they missed one night, they would call each other on the next evening.

He looked at his watch after he parked in the parking lot for the sheriff's department. He knew Leroy was in a meeting from seven thirty to eight thirty. Once inside the office complex, he headed to the coffee machine. Levi was standing there and stirring a spoon in his cup.

Quinn said, "So, how is Carroll County's most eligible bachelor doing today?"

"McSpain, some days are better than others. But, dang, I'm always happy to be me!"

They both laughed, failing to notice Leroy and another person coming up from behind. "Well, now, isn't it grand to have two of my favorite people being all happy while the rest of us are hard at work?"

They all laughed, and Leroy said to Quinn, "Have you met Brad Frank? He is the editor of the *Galax Gazette.*"

Quinn stuck out his right hand. "Well, no, I haven't, but I certainly read the *Galax Gazette*. Good to keep up to date with all the local happenings."

Brad shook Quinn's hand. "You're too kind, Quinn. Keeping our readers informed and listening to the readers who will never like anything we print are always interesting tasks."

Leroy looked at Quinn. "So, do you have the picture you told me about?"

Quinn reached into his pocket. "I do."

"Good. Let's go into my office, and we all will have a look at it." Brad looked at the sheriff. "Yes, you come along too, Brad, 'cause you might recognize the face as well."

They all sat at the round table in Leroy's office and listened to Quinn tell them how and where the picture was taken. Levi and the sheriff looked at it together. They looked at each other and shook their heads. Levi scratched his head. "That's a rough picture, but it doesn't look like anybody I've run into."

Levi passed the picture to Brad. He scrutinized it for a minute, and then he looked at the sheriff. "This is a rough picture, but from what I see, I think I know who this is."

All ears in the room pricked up; all eyes focused on Brad. He looked at them all. "I'm pretty sure this is Tommie Cruz. He lives in downtown Galax. I see him at Macado's from time to time, but I really don't know that much about him. Heck, I don't even know what he does for a living."

Just as the sheriff was about to say something, his secretary knocked on the door and poked her head in. "Sheriff, I hate to bother you, but a woman is calling from some place called Rodanthe, North Carolina, and she is saying she needs to talk with you about a possible murder in Galax."

All four looked at each other, and then Leroy said, "Transfer the call, and I will put it on speakerphone."

Within a moment, the red light on the phone sitting on his conference table lighted up. Leroy punched the button. "Hello, this is Sheriff Jefferson. With whom am I speaking?"

There was a pause on the other end. "Sheriff, this is Claire Kelly, and I live in the Outer Banks of North Carolina, in a town called Rodanthe. My best girlfriend, Missy Brereton, who lives in Galax, visited me a while back for a short vacation. Well, I just received a letter from her that was very disturbing. She asked me to call her to see if she was all right. I did, but her cell phone is no longer in service. I then tried calling the hardware store where she works, and they told me she hasn't been in.

"Her note then instructed me to call you and tell you that a person named Tommie Cruz was responsible for trying to kill the FBI woman. Now, Sheriff, all this is very frightening to me, so I hope it means something to you."

All four men sat in stunned silence in the room.

The voice on the phone came alive. "Are you still there, Sheriff?"

Levi looked at the speakerphone. "I am, Claire. I'm just trying to sort out what you just told me. Listen, I'm going to call the sheriff in your area, which I think is Dare County, and have a deputy go to your residence to secure the letter. We will then call the Galax Police Department and have them start looking for your friend. If you hear from Missy in any way, shape, or form, though, call me immediately."

"I will, Sheriff, and I pray Missy is OK and that you find her soon!" she said, and then she hung up.

They all looked at each other, and Levi said, "Who the fuck is Tommie Cruz? I have never heard of him."

Leroy went to his desk and turned his computer on. As soon as he typed the name "Tommie Cruz," the search engine churned for a moment, and the results were eventually posted on the screen. He quickly scrolled through some of the results.

"Shit," said the sheriff. "Not a damn hit for any Tommie Cruz in Galax or anywhere in Virginia, for that matter. I'll send an e-mail to Chief Clarkston at Galax to see if they know any Tommie Cruz. Levi, get to your desk. Do a complete search in the system of the National Crime Information Center for that name."

Quinn was pecking away on his new iPhone 7 Plus and looked perplexed. "I am not getting any hits on this guy either. I can't even tell where he lives in Galax. It's as if he doesn't exist."

However, some seven miles away, in downtown Galax, Tommie Cruz did exist. He was sitting in his secluded operations room, and he was watching all the systems he had hacked in order to place sleeping malware, which was now coming to life.

Any search on his name sent messages back to him with copies of the inquiries. His screens lit up with all the inquiries from the sheriff's department to the Galax Police Department to the Virginia State Police.

Tommie was stunned that he was now the center of attention. He knew he had to act fast because the police would soon be knocking on his door. He set his emergency plan in place, which destroyed all the information he could not carry on his storage sticks.

He took prepacked bags of clothing and weapons out of a closet and loaded them into the back seat of his truck. When he finished, he checked, closed, and locked all the doors of his house. He then opened a private app on his phone and armed the booby traps.

As he turned off Main Street, he looked in his rearview mirror, knowing he would never see Galax again. He also knew his only focus was to kill Quinn McSpain and Sheriff Leroy Jefferson... *no matter what*!

☆ ☆ ☆

Tanya Torres crossed the river in a canoe at her usual time on Monday. Judy Klassen was waiting for her and the other two women she picked up. Tanya was like a daughter to Judy, and she thought the world of her.

The usual Monday-morning pleasantries were exchanged among the women as they drove to the lodge. Tanya got out at the restaurant, and Judy drove the other two to the top of the hill, where they cleaned the cabins before they went down and cleaned the lodge.

Tanya spent the day working with Hope and the other women at the restaurant. She was surprised to see Hannah, who had come down from school to have lunch with Hope. As the day wore on, Tanya Torres knew what she must do.

Judy came down to the restaurant prior to closing. She noticed Tanya looked ill at ease. "What is the matter, my dear? What is troubling you?" Judy asked.

Tanya looked at her. "I need to talk with you and Pastor John. It is very important!"

Judy sensed that Tanya had something to say. She took her hand, and they walked up the hill to the lodge. Pastor John was in his office when they entered. He turned to look at them both.

"John, I think Tanya has something to tell us," said Judy.

John motioned them to sit near his desk. He asked Tanya, "What is troubling you, my child?"

Tanya lowered her head and began speaking in a hushed tone. "I am so frightened. Yesterday, two men from the cartel and two men from Virginia came to our house. The men from Virginia are here to kill Hope and Hannah."

John sat back in his chair. "That is serious, Tanya. When do they plan to come here?"

"They are coming tomorrow. Early in the morning. Before the sun comes up. Only the four of them will come. I don't want anyone to be killed."

Pastor John stood and hugged her as she cried. "Do not worry, Tanya. We will do what we can to make sure the mother and daughter are protected. Now, go back home, and tell those men that everything is normal. We will all be OK. You did the right thing by warning us."

Judy took her hand and led her to her truck. She then drove her to the river's edge and the waiting canoe.

Judy looked at her and hugged her before she left. "We will all be OK. We love you."

Tanya got into the canoe and gently paddled across the river. She shuddered at the thought of seeing Suarez and Larios *on the other side.*

☆ ☆ ☆

Quinn drove with the sheriff on the way to downtown Galax. Levi followed in his own car. It didn't take long before they were in the parking lot of the Galax Police Department. The lot was filling up with other local and Virginia State Police vehicles.

Leroy saw Chief Clarkston after they entered the building. He waved Leroy and Quinn into his office. Leroy introduced Quinn to the chief, and then everyone sat down. The chief said, "Well, Leroy, we know where he lives. It's practically under our nose here on Main Street. I have two officers watching the front and back entrances.

"From what they tell me, it looks as if he uses the back entrance from the alley. They see that a few lights are on, and they hear music playing. The apartment that Missy lives in is right across from the alley, but there doesn't appear to be anyone there."

Leroy looked at him. "I bet you already had someone go to the courthouse to get a search warrant, didn't you?"

"It's on its way, Leroy. Now, we are going to head over there with the SWAT team of the state police and surprise Mr. Tommie Cruz with a visit."

They all headed out the door to the parking lot at the back. Quinn counted some fifteen SWAT officers, along with six Galax police officers. They took the backstreet that allowed them to cross over into the back alley.

When they were all in place, Chief Clarkston took a final tug on the straps of his bulletproof vest. Quinn and Leroy were in the background. They were watching the police officers take their assigned places. At that very moment, Leroy's cell phone rang.

He looked at it and saw his wife, Laneisha, was calling. He knew that was unusual because she never called unless something was wrong. He punched the answer button. "Hey, what's up, Laneisha? I'm in the middle of something."

He could barely hear her faint voice. "Leroy, a man is here at our house, and he will kill me if you and Quinn don't come here now. Alone. He said his name is *Tommie.*"

☆ ☆ ☆

Louisa slowly opened her eyes. Her throbbing headache reminded her of the perils of drinking too much moonshine.

The empty spot beside her in the bed told her Badgett was already up and out of the room.

The tension in her mind added to her overall discomfort. Her mind drifted back to her encounter with Badgett on the dock. While she hated herself for what she did, she sensed a very strong attraction to this man, and that frightened her.

Even more disturbing was that it went beyond the physical magnetism between them. She enjoyed just being with him. She tried her best to muffle the tiny voice in her head that was telling her she was infatuated with this younger man, who seemed to be attracted to her.

Then again, she was lonely without Quinn by her side. The pounding in her head grew louder as she sat on the side of the bed. She stood and saw she was wearing his T-shirt. She looked around the cabin but did not see him anywhere.

She took a few steps to the front door and saw him standing in the shallow part of the lake. He was holding a bar of soap and washing himself from top to bottom. He saw her watching. "Hey, come on down here and help me. I need some help with some special places."

Louisa flipped him the bird. "No way, Prince Charming. I need some coffee, and I need it right now."

She turned and went back into the cabin. She sat at the table and was lost in thought, but she was enjoying every sip of the strong coffee he had made. Who was this man she had only met a month ago? The porch stairs creaked as he came onto the porch and into the house. He had a towel wrapped around his waist.

"Well, look at that naughty girl enjoying some of my chicory coffee. I thought you were going to sleep all day. We have got to do some fishing today."

Louisa was about to answer when Badgett's phone rang. He looked at the display. "It's John." He hit the answer button. "Hello, John."

There was a slight pause. "Badgett, is Louisa with you?"

He looked at Louisa. "Why, yes, she is. We are at the lake."

John took a moment. "I need the both of you to get back here right now. Something urgent has developed."

"We will be there in twenty minutes," said Badgett, and he ended the call.

Louisa was sipping her coffee and waiting patiently.

"Get dressed as fast as you can," said Badgett. "John needs us at the lodge. Something must be happening."

Louisa took the final sip, put her cup down, and headed to the bedroom to dress.

Within minutes, they were on Badgett's motorcycle and heading back to the lodge. Louisa held on tightly, leaning forward and whispering in his ear, "What was last night all about? I really have to know."

Without changing his expression, Badgett cocked his head back and replied, "It was only sex. *Nothing more.*"

CHAPTER 22

Quinn followed Leroy as he walked away from the alley and back toward the police department. Quinn caught up with him and asked, "What was that all about, Leroy? Who was that on the phone?"

Leroy picked up the pace as Quinn joined him at his side. "It was Laneisha. That motherfucker has her hostage in my house, and he only wants to see me and you."

As Leroy and Quinn reached Leroy's car, Chief Clarkston gave the order to break down the back door. He followed the very first SWAT officer in through the door. He barely heard the officer scream, "Booby trap!"

Those were the last words Chief Clarkston ever heard.

As Quinn opened the passenger door to Leroy's car, the sound of the explosion in the alley was deafening. Everything around them shook. He slid in as best he could, and Leroy shut his door and started the car.

Leroy wasted no time heading out of the parking lot and back to Highway 58. He was heading west to Hillsville. They encountered fire trucks and ambulances already responding to the explosion.

Leroy looked forward as he said, "Why just you and me, Quinn? What does this motherfucker want from us?"

Quinn looked straight ahead as well. "Leroy, I don't have a clue, but we are going to find out real soon."

Within minutes, Leroy slowed down as he approached his home's driveway. He came to a stop some twenty feet from his house. Just as he did, his cell phone rang. Laneisha's name was on the screen. He waited a moment before he pushed the button.

"Sheriff, I hope it's just you and McSpain in that car. Now, both of you get out, and take your shirts and your belts off. And you better not have any ankle holsters on."

They both stepped out of the car and did what Tommie had instructed. They stood there for a moment, and then they heard a voice call from the front door. "Walk toward me slowly. With your hands up high."

Leroy led the way up the stairs, and Quinn was close behind.

They entered the kitchen and found Laneisha tied to a chair. Her mouth was gagged. Tommie emerged from around the corner with a sawed-off shotgun, and he regarded them. He also had a 357 magnum in a holster he was wearing. He smiled a wicked smile.

Leroy looked at Laneisha. "Did he hurt you, baby?"

She shook her head.

"Jefferson, I didn't hurt her. Not yet. You are the two motherfuckers I'm going to kill; then I will have my way with your black-ass wife."

Quinn looked at him. “Pardon me for asking, but who the fuck are you? I don’t believe we have ever done anything to harm you. Have we?”

Tommie pulled two chairs around. “Sit down,” he ordered.

They did as he asked.

Tommie kept his shotgun trained on Laneisha’s head. He threw two sets of handcuffs to Quinn. “Cuff the sheriff and then yourself, and don’t try any funny stuff, or I’ll blow her brains out.”

Quinn did as he said, never taking his eyes off Tommie. He sat motionless after he cuffed himself. Tommie relaxed when Quinn finished. He pulled a chair up and sat in front of them. “You two have no clue who I am, do you? You can’t imagine how long I have been waiting to avenge what you did. You know I’m going to kill you both, but first I want you to understand why you two fuckers are going to die.” Tommie stood, walked over to Leroy, and slapped him in the face. “You are the motherfucker who pulled the trigger that sent my father to his grave.”

A blank stare came over Leroy’s face. He still could not connect Tommie to anyone.

Quinn was mentally narrowing down the options when it suddenly hit him. “You are somehow connected to Father Tony, aren’t you? He was a priest, though. He didn’t have any children. As far as we knew.”

Tommie spun around, walked over to Quinn, and looked at him. “See? That wasn’t so hard after all, was it? Pity you are so smart only during the last moments of your life.”

He backhanded Quinn across the face after he finished speaking.

Leroy spit blood on the floor. "Listen, you only want us. Leave my wife out of this. She had nothing to do with that bastard I killed."

Tommie walked over to Leroy and hit him again. "Father Tony adopted me when I had nothing. He sent me to college and cared for me like a real father. I loved that man. He was never as vicious as you claimed."

Quinn squirmed in his chair, but he could hardly move. Tommie sat in his chair and looked at all three of them. His eyes settled on Quinn. "I'm going to kill you first, McSpain, but I'm going to shoot you several times. That way, you'll suffer. Then I'm going to torture your wife, Jefferson. After you have seen it all, I will put you out of your misery."

He picked up his sawed-off shotgun and walked over to Quinn. He brought it up to Quinn's head and whispered, "Think a good thought, motherfucker. It will be your last!"

Quinn, Leroy, and Laneisha closed their eyes. The blast was immediate, and the sound was deafening. Quinn was knocked out of his chair. Tommie fell to the floor and into Quinn's lap. Part of Tommie's head was missing.

Quinn jerked his head back to look in the direction of a shattered window. He realized that Tommie had been killed by someone standing outside the window. Within a moment, Levi's smiling face peered through the broken glass.

Levi looked at the three faces staring in disbelief at him. "Here's Levi!" he yelled while holding up his 9 mm pistol.

He then ran around to the door and came into the kitchen. He untied Laneisha and took the gag from her mouth. He then freed the sheriff and Quinn.

Leroy had tears welling up in his eyes. "God dammit, Levi Blackburn, I have never been so happy to see you! How in God's name did you find us here?"

"Well, I saw you and Quinn leave the scene in Galax. I figured something was mighty important for you two to high-tail it out of Galax. So, I followed you and soon realized you were heading home. Well, I parked in the puckerbush and watched you both get undressed by your car. I found that a little strange, so I waited a bit before I sneaked up to that window. I waited and listened awhile 'cause I needed to hear what that ole boy had to say.

"So, when I figured he was about to shoot Quinn, I took aim and put that bastard out of his misery. That prick killed Chief Clarkston and a few other officers when he blew up the building he had lived in."

Quinn walked over to him. "Levi, I never realized you're that good of a shot!"

Levi blushed a bit and looked at him. Before he could say anything, Leroy looked at Quinn. "*He's not!*"

✲ ✲ ✲

The time had come for Estrada and the others to cross the river. Arrangements had been made for a truck to be parked on the other side. They knew they would arrive on the other side an hour or two before dawn. Tanya had drawn a map of the cabin where Hope and Hannah would be sleeping.

They also knew where the airstrip was located. Suarez thought that if all hell broke loose, the Mennonites might try to fly the woman and her daughter out of any danger.

As soon as they loaded the truck with their weapons, they slowly drove toward the lodge. They wore camouflage fatigues, and their faces were painted black. They had earpieces to communicate with each other. Near the entrance, they parked the truck and slowly walked up the hill. They made their way toward the cabins.

When they were by the cabin they thought Hope and Hannah were in, Estrada and Medina slowly pushed the door open. Inside, they found the bedroom and saw the two beds were occupied. Estrada fired two rounds into each bed. His silencer muffled the noise of the shots.

They waited a second for any movement in the beds, but there was none. Estrada pulled back the covers, only to see two small mannequins dressed in nightclothes. "Fuck," he mumbled, and he backed out of the cabin.

They stopped in their tracks when they saw Suarez and Larios lying on the ground. They weren't moving. Medina bent down and looked at them. They were garroted. Estrada spun around to see a man looking at him—Pastor John.

"Put down your weapons," said the pastor, "or you'll end up like your friends."

Pastor John was holding a submachine gun.

Medina aimed his pistol at the pastor and fired twice. Both shots hit him in the chest. Estrada turned and started to run down the hill. Medina knew they were running toward the airfield.

Badgett had finished fueling up the Cessna 206. Louisa had packed all of Hope and Hannah's things in the plane, as well as both of the women. She stepped back and took out her satellite phone. She dialed Ben Robert's number. He answered on the second ring.

"Ben, this is Louisa. We are flying out right now. The heat is on, and we need to get out. Meet us at the airport in Belize."

She never got a chance to say another word because the phone was knocked from her hand. She never heard the shot.

She crouched down and crawled to the other side of the plane. She stood, only to feel the cold steel of a gun barrel push against her ear. Medina smiled as he began to pull the trigger. He never saw Badgett approach. Badgett's knife slit his throat.

Medina dropped to the ground without ever getting the shot off. Badgett spun around to see Estrada moving toward the plane's door. Estrada started to climb in but reacted to Louisa's shot, which went through his kneecap. He fell to the ground but rolled and aimed at Badgett. He squeezed off a round that missed Badgett's head by inches.

Louisa shot again before Estrada could get off another round. Her shot was true and hit him between his eyes. Badgett rolled them both away from the plane. He looked at Louisa. "Let's get out of here. There might be more."

Louisa climbed in the plane, and Badgett followed, closing the door behind him. Within minutes, he taxied out onto the airstrip and had the plane airborne in no time. John looked up at the plane. He was on top of the hill, and Judy was by his side. They were both happy—especially because his vest had stopped the bullets.

Louisa sat next to Hannah on the plane as it rose above the morning clouds. Hannah looked at Louisa and asked, "Are we going to be all right, Aunt Louisa?"

"Yes, Hannah. We are all safe now. It's time to take you home."

Louisa then sat in silence and wondered what had happened to her in the past few weeks. Her life had been turned upside down. She looked at Badgett behind the controls of the plane and couldn't deny the feelings she had for him. She didn't think her love for Quinn had diminished in any way, but she was torn by her feelings for this younger man. She wasn't looking forward to the moment when she would have to tell Quinn.

The mere notion that another man could come into her life and challenge her love for Quinn was confusing. The joy she felt for Hope and Hannah was muffled by the angst of her confusion.

In no time, Badgett was communicating with the tower at the airport in Belize. After he was cleared to land, he quickly set the wheels on the ground and taxied up to a private hangar. Louisa looked out the window and saw Ben Roberts standing in the doorway.

Louisa was the last to leave the plane. Roberts took her aside and said, "I just spoke with the Belize Defence Force. They identified Estrada and Medina among the four who were killed in Blue Creek. I've already notified Jeannie Wishart in Virginia. It's safe for you to go home."

Louisa gave him a hug, and then she helped Hope and Hannah board the DEA jet in the hangar. She looked at the Cessna as Badgett opened the door. She ran over and held the door open before he could close it. "So, not even so much as a good-bye?" she asked.

He looked into her eyes. "Louisa, forget about me. Go back to your life."

She held the door. "I'm having a problem with that. You are very special to me."

Badgett pulled the door free and closed it but not before saying, "It was only sex. Get back to your life, and forget about me."

Louisa backed away and watched him taxi onto the runway and lift off into the blue sky. She turned and walked toward the jet *with a heavy heart.*

✫ ✫ ✫

Elva Estrada reached for her cell phone and did not recognize the number on the screen. She was concerned because Estrada had not called in several days. She answered the call.

"Elva, this is Eric Torres in La Union. I have very bad news for you. Both Duke and Roger are dead. I'm so sorry."

She thanked Torres and suggested the bodies be taken care of in La Union. Once she hung up, she looked at Maria Medina and Tony Esquivel. "They are both dead."

Maria looked at her. "So, what do we do now?"

Esquivel did not hesitate. "We must get out of here and get out now. Once the word gets out that Duke and Roger are dead, they will come for us and kill us. We cannot waste any time. Pack as little as you can. I will take care of the computer files."

No less than an hour later, the three of them left the compound in Esquivel's truck. As they turned the corner, Elva looked out the window and was taken aback. Tiller was watching them leave, and Elva was certain the witch was smiling.

Tiller slowly walked in through the open gate and walked to the barn. She quickly found what she was looking for. There was no doubt the five gallons of gasoline would get the job done.

Within ten minutes, the nearest volunteer fire department got the call of the massive conflagration. Tiller was halfway back up the mountain when she turned to *watch it burn.*

* * *

The DEA jet landed in Greensboro, and after the jet taxied to a stop, it was met by one car. Jeannie Wishart greeted Hope and Hannah and hugged Louisa. The three of them told their stories to Jeannie as they drove back to Hillsville.

Wishart dropped Hope and Hannah off at Pastor Kauffmann's house. The amount of joy the mother, daughter, and Kauffmanns shared was overwhelming. Wishart then drove Louisa to Quinn's house. He was waiting on the porch when they pulled into the driveway.

Louisa exchanged good-byes with Jeannie, who then left. Quinn took Louisa's bags into the house. He came back into the kitchen and gave her a long hug. "God, I am so thankful you are home safe."

Louisa looked at him. "Jeannie filled me in on what you and Leroy went through on this end. That was terrible!"

"Hey, the most important thing is that we are both alive and together again. I can't tell you how much I missed you! God, I love you, woman!"

He went over to the wine rack and pulled out a bottle. He had the cork out in one swift pull, and he filled two glasses. He took one to Louisa on the couch and noticed she was crying. "Hey, what's wrong? Are you hurt?"

Louisa wiped the tears from her eyes and blurted, "Quinn, something happened in Belize. I never thought I could, but I became attracted to another man."

She cried harder, and Quinn pulled back a bit and looked at her. "Tell me what happened."

Louisa took a sip of wine and thought for a moment before she began. She interrupted herself by sobbing between her words. She left nothing out. After she finished, she blurted, "Quinn, I didn't mean to hurt you!"

He stood and looked at her. "Look at me. Do you love him?"

Louisa shook her head. "I'm not sure. It's all so confusing."

Quinn set his wine down and walked around the room. He looked at her. "Listen, I can't live with you if you aren't all in. It isn't fair to me, and it isn't fair to you. So, I'm leaving to go to Winston-Salem for a bit. Pack your things, and be gone when I get back. Go wherever you need to go to sort all this out. But don't come back before you do!"

With that, he turned, took his keys, and walked out the door. He pounded his steering wheel as he drove away, and tears streamed down his cheeks.

CHAPTER 23

The sun was setting when he pulled back into his driveway. Louisa's Volvo was gone. He unlocked the door and went to the kitchen. On the table was the extra set of keys she used. The keys were sitting on an envelope.

He slowly opened the envelope and removed the single sheet of paper. He unfolded it and began reading.

> Quinn,
> No person on earth means more to me than you do, *but...*

Made in the USA
Middletown, DE
06 March 2017